WHEN DREAMS CHANGE

JORDYN MERYL

Published by jm dragonfly, L.L.C.
Des Moines, IA
Copyright © April 2012 Jordyn Meryl

ISBN-13: 978-1475150230
ISBN-10: 1475150237

First Printing: April 2012
Printed in the United States of America
Cover Design-EJR Digital Art-www.ejrdigitalart.com
Author photograph-Trish Toma-Lark

Other Books
By
Jordyn Meryl

Italian Dream Series

When Dreams Change-Book 1

When Dreams Collide-Book 2

When Dreams Die-Books 3

Becca's Dance
The journey of life is not about the path traveled, but
the dance

The Trouble With Angels

Home Before Dark

The Space Between-A Paranormal Romantic Suspense

Coming Soon

Katie's Wind

Silent Running

CHAPTER ONE

"You stupid-cheating-mother-fucking-son-of-a-bitch!"

The heavy stoneware plate hurled from Jessica's hand headed towards her husband.

Sweat lingered over her eyebrows running into her sea green eyes. She was so infuriated she didn't even pause to wipe it away.

Charles, her middle-aged, non-athletic nerd of a husband, darted to his right at the last second. The plate hit the wall behind his head shattering into pieces. Raising his hands out in front of him to block her onslaught, his wire-rimmed glasses twisted on his nose.

"Damn it, Jessica. Buying the café was a mistake. I just can't stay here and work all the time. I feel stifled."

Her words came at him in a blaze of pure rage. "What the hell do you mean, mistake? We sold everything we owned to get the money to buy this café."

"Well, I just don't think this business venture is going to work." Charles stood with his arms still up in a defensive block.

Jessica grabbed two more plates, angrily launching one. "What do you mean it's not going to work?" Charles dodged the first plate.

Her voice seethed with white fury. "What's the real reason, Charles?" The second plate soared at high speed. It nicked his forehead, just above his eye. Blood oozed from the cut.

"Fuck this! Okay. I want someone else. Bambi and I want a life together." He held his hand over the wound. "Enough! I'm leaving. It's all yours honey. Do whatever the hell you want. I'm done, finished, out of here."

With another plate in her hand, Jessica watched as Charles twisted around and did a hasty escape out the door. Blonde Bambi was waiting for him outside. Dragging his little sex kitten behind him, Charles exited indubitably from her life.

Jessica's anger was so fierce she could have killed the no-good-rat bastard. A hand on her wrist stopped her from throwing the last plate.

Josh, her fourteen year old busboy, said in his thick Italian accent. "Excuse me, Signora, but we need the dishes to serve the food."

The simple words brought her outburst to an end. Jessica slammed the plate down hard on the counter, breaking it anyway. It was the last straw. Unacceptable tears streamed down her face as she leaned on the counter. The pain of the plate pieces cutting her elbows hurt worse than losing a cheating husband.

What am I going to do?

Her husband had just walked out on her with a young "boob for brains" bimbo and left her with a new restaurant, a stack of bills, and no money. On the edge of thirty-five, she wasn't prepared for this change in her life, plus she was in way-the-hell-n'-gone-Italy.

The bus boy spoke quietly, with his voice holding back a quiver. "Signora? Josh had shown up at the restaurant's door one day, willing to work to help out his family. Her heart was instantly taken by the sweet faced youth, and he had proven to be a hard worker and wise way beyond his years. He was one of the few employees whom Jessica had liked. Charles had hired the rest.

Jessica tried to keep her voice kind. "Yes, Josh?" She wiped her eyes on the sleeve of her shirt.

"We open in thirty minutes."

"Oh, shit." Jessica twirled around and surveyed the restaurant. Opened only a week, the business was good, with several customers becoming patrons. But Charles was her bartender. She could not be a hostess, oversee the kitchen, and tend bar at the same time. The stool caught her as she plopped down.

"What am I going to do?" Her words were said out loud. Embarrassed, she looked over at Josh trying to act as if she hadn't meant to speak.

Josh stood wide-eyed in front of her. "How can I help?"

Jessica chuckled. "Can you tend bar?"

"No, but I have a cousin who is a barista."

Jessica snapped around to look at him. "A what?" She still didn't have a complete handle on the Italian language.

The young bus boy searched for the right word. "A bar. . .person.

He had her attention now. "Seriously?"

"Si."

So overjoyed at having a possible solution to one problem, Jessica jumped up and hugged him. "Call him." She dug deep to get her cell phone out of her apron pocket.

"I don't know how to call him, but I know where he is."

"Go. Get him. Now!"

As Josh left out the front door, Jessica surveyed her little restaurant. Checkered table clothes, candles in wine bottles and a single daisy in cut glass vases decorated each table. The space was laid out in close quarters. The dining room held ten small tables; the bar stood in one corner. Stairs at the side of the bar led to the apartment upstairs. The modest space drew her to the quaintness of the café. On the waterfront, the large windows beaconed her to come enjoy a good meal, a bottle of wine, a quiet time. Between the dining room and the kitchen, hung a swinging metal door. The activity of the kitchen could be seen and heard to the very front. She liked that, it created an atmosphere of intimacy.

She and Charles had sold everything they could to pursue the dream of owning a small trattoria in Italy, *Di Me Sogni*. Their jobs in New York had been high-powered, high-stress positions. Tired of the rat race, they came to the Mediterranean to live by the sea. It was a lot of work to get the restaurant up and running. However, she had believed working together they could live their dream. Now half of the dream's working part just walked out the door.

Damn you all to hell, Charles!

Shards of stoneware littered the tile floor. Jessica stood, walked behind the bar. Grabbing the broom and dust pan, she went to mess she had created. Sweeping up the smashed plates, she couldn't help but smile as she remembered one bouncing off his head.

Glad I drew blood.

The plate pieces in the dustpan made a tinkling sound as she dumped them in the trash can.

Carrying the broom, dustpan and trash can into the kitchen, she nodded to the staff who had no doubt heard her angry outburst. Leaning the broom and dustpan against a wall, she carried the trash can out the door to the big bin.

The damaged dinnerware fell and bounced against the metal sides. She stood for a moment thinking of how it represented her broken life. Her husband had just left her for another woman.

Woman?

She doubted Bambi was old enough to drink in the States.

Let it go. What's done is done.

Now her focus needed to be about surviving on her wits alone. She could do this.

The noise of a small scooter grew louder behind her. As she turned, Josh rounded the corner of the building alone.

Damn! No cousin!

Josh's face was expressionless as he puttered up to her. She pasted a smile on her face; she knew he had tried to help. Placing a hand on his shoulder, she started to speak.

The roar of a motorcycle shook the ground under her as a young man in black appeared in the narrow alleyway. A black helmet covered his face except for his dark eyes shining through the opening. The shadowy, mysterious stranger stopped just behind Josh. Jessica's eyes were riveted on his body as he dismounted the bike.

"This is Alejandro, my cousin." Josh looked up at her.

As Alejandro took off his helmet, tucking it under his arm, he removed one black leather glove leisurely one-finger-at-a-time, his gaze locked on Jessica's.

Alejandro extended his hand to Jessica, "Signorina." His voice, as well as his touch, flowed hot like molten lava. His body bent down as his mouth touched her hand in a delightful, sensual kiss.

Jessica's voice barely came out of her throat. "It's Signora, but..."

For how long?

"...Signorina is fine." His touch still lingered as he released her hand.

Alejandro's smile lit up his face, revealing perfect white teeth. "Somebody's loss I fear."

Jessica caught the interaction as he side-glanced Josh. Josh shook his head. Well, Josh would have explained why she needed a bartender on a moment's notice.

There were no secrets.

Jessica slightly lifted her long skirt to keep from tripping, "Follow me." Stepping between them, she hoped they were behind her, but did not look back. As Jessica entered the building, the kitchen workers all turned in unison towards her, pity for her on their faces.

Nope, no secrets here.

Head held high, Jessica marched all the way through the kitchen, straight into the dining room across to the bar. Whipping around quickly only to come face-to-face with Alejandro, his warm, rich smell of soap and leather filled her senses, she stepped back bumping a stool.

Taking a stand with her feet planted firmly, she addressed him as his boss. "This is the bar."

Duh.

"You know what to do with everything here?"

Again with the smile, he looked around, ran his ungloved hand along the rich wood of the counter. "Si. I know exactly what to do..." He winked at her. "...with everything."

Stay on course here, girl.

"You've bartended before?"

"Si." His dark, enchanting eyes mixed with mischief.

"Where?" She didn't really care, but didn't want him to think her irresponsible by not asking some questions, after all, he would be working for her alone.

My first post-Charles hire.

"Many places. I am putting myself through college tending bar. I get good tips."

Oh, I just bet you do.

"College? For what?" In the best unassuming poise as she could muster, she leaned against the bar.

He was removing his leather jacket, showing broad shoulders under a thin white shirt. He rolled up his sleeves to reveal deep caramel forearms. Tight muscles pushed at his skin.

"Pre-med." He took the black apron from the counter, tied it around his lean waist, and looked up at Jessica. "Let me take care of everything." He picked up the bottles of liquor one by one reading the labels. "Good stuff. Expensive. Quality."

Yeah, if Charles was anything he wasn't cheap.

Jessica quietly walked around the bar. "Alejandro, thank you. You're saving my ass tonight."

He looked around her, a smile twitched at the corner of his mouth. "Nice ass. Well worth saving."

The blush tingling at her face bordered on a hot flash.

Damn!

The little café was filling with customers, so she went to greet them. As she walked towards the door to unlock it, she re-straightened the already straight chairs and rearranged picture perfect flowers. Jessica took a deep breath.

I can do this. I will do this. Charles, you no good shit ass!

After seating her first customers and handing them a menu, she glanced at the bar. Alejandro was already busy arranging the glasses and putting fresh baked garlic bread chips on the counter. As if he felt her eyes, he looked up and winked again. Her confidence soared. She could do this.

* * *

The hours flew by when Jessica realized it was a little before nine o'clock. The typical tourist rush had slacked off. Now the place was empty, except for one couple in the corner, who only had eyes for each other.

The Europeans crowd would begin filtering in, as they ate dinner later. From now until midnight the crowd would be steady, lingering over their meals. Jessica felt the worst of her first night alone was behind her.

Time for a short break. Jessica meandered over to the quiet bar to watch Alejandro's back as he cleaned and arranged bottles. She sat down on one of the stools and leaned her elbows on the bar.

His graceful movements and precise way he organized the bar looked as if he was settling in. Glancing at the brandy glass holding his tips, she noticed it was full, with several of the bills being tens and twenties.

The women customers noticed the new bartender right away. No one asked about Charles. Just praise for the drinks as very good and the bartender as very handsome, a nice addition.

Alejandro turned around, a smile spread slowly over his face as he leaned on the bar. Leaning towards her, he spoke close enough for Jessica's neck to feel his breath.

"How's it going pretty Signorina?" His words tore at her beat up soul.

Pretty. How pretty could you be if your husband left you for someone younger?

"Grateful you were here. I think we had more people tonight than any other night." She put her hand on his arm. "Thank you."

He glanced down at her hand, then back up to her eyes. "It was my pleasure."

Jessica slid her hand from his arm, moving slightly back so she was not so close to him. He straightened up, wiped the bar with a towel, his eyes on her. His actions were slow and hypnotic.

"Signorina Jessica." His soft, sexy tone made her look just at him. The rest of the café faded away. "You are a strong, beautiful woman. Your husband will come back. He would be a fool not to."

The words felt like cold water thrown in her face.

"I don't want him back. He's a fool."

She knew she had raised her voice an octave. She glanced around the room. The couple in the corner had ignored her, the wait staff was in the kitchen.

As she got up, she lowly murmured to herself. "No good, son-of-a-bitch. He can go to hell. I can do just fine without him." Glancing up at Alejandro, her anger rose as she saw him leaning against the counter, grinning at her. "I can." Convincing herself, as much as him.

He lowered his head in agreement. "You will."

With a firm nod, she started for the kitchen. She stopped short, turned, shuffled back to Alejandro. Her hand grabbed the front of his shirt, bringing him into her, she whispered in his ear.

"Will you work for me, please?" Looking up again she saw the smile.

He leaned in and whispered, soft and easy against her hair. "I will."

"And college?" His shirt felt silky on her chin.

His chest shook with quiet laughter. "I'm between semesters right now."

Biting her lower lip, she asked the question she should have asked four hours ago. "How much do you want paid?"

His chuckle tickled her ear. "What did you pay the other guy?"

She leaned back to see his face. "Nothing. He was my now long-gone husband."

He looked up over her head, as a grin played around his sexy mouth. When he looked back at her, his words were touched with humor. "Well, I guess the standard rate for a bartender plus tips will work for now."

"Well, okay." She released his shirt, patted his chest. "I can now make my exit."

With a swish of her hips she walked away, proud of herself for handling her first business deal. Her long skirt rustled around her ankles. Her dangling earrings brushed her jaw.

Charles always thought he was the big dealer, because he had worked on Wall Street. Well, her marketing skills were going to get her through this.

And endless hours of working my ass off. The dream I had for this café will live on, even if some things have to change.

* * *

With the café closed and everyone gone, Jessica locked the back door. Her former rage subsided as she grabbed the wooden railing of the back stairs. Totally exhausted, she trudged her work weary body up the stairs to the living quarters above the café.

The rush of late night customers had seemed heavier than normal. Alejandro had handled the bar with expert precision and charm. He was going to be a good asset to her little business, not to mention her scenery; he certainly was nice to look at. As she entered her small apartment, she flipped on the light.

Yeah, a little eye candy, is okay.

For tonight, she was done. Going in the bathroom, she shed her clothes. Standing naked, she looked in the mirror while brushing her teeth. Her reflection showed a less uptight Jessica; she was too tired to keep her anger going. Pulling on boxers and a tank, she padded to her bed. The smooth, cool sheets welcomed her fatigued and beat-up spirit and body.

Her wrath at Charles' leaving was more about his deserting the dream and less about his leaving her. She wanted this café to make it so badly. It had taken them both two years of saving, planning, and determination to get to this point. Then, in less than a month, the stupid shit screwed around on her and walked out.

As she stretched out an absurd thought crossed her mind.

I have the whole bed to myself.

She kicked her legs under the covers, spread eagle.

Ahhhh.

Staring up at the stucco ceiling, she thought back to how mad she had been. She chuckled at the thought of dishes flying through the air, the outrageous frenzy that had blinded her.

Got him good, didn't I?

She curled her body, bringing her knees to her chest. Tears rushed from her eyes covering her cheeks, on down her neck. Burying her face in the pillow, she felt her body shake. For the first time all day she released all the hurt, anger and resentment she had shoved down.

You bastard! You will rue the day you crossed me.

She pounded the mattress with her fists, allowing herself to cry it out. When there were no more tears, she lay on her back and stared out the skylight at the night sky.

Enough. Save the energy for making sure you accomplish your plans. For now, they're your plans, Charles is no longer part of them.

Sleep stealthily began to move over her. Tomorrow she would have to face reality.

You're on your own, girlfriend!

CHAPTER TWO

The soothing sound of waves crashing on the rocks outside her window woke Jessica the next morning. She allowed her body to enjoy a long, leisurely stretch. Sunbeams sparkled across the end of her bed. The sea breeze left the taste of salt on her lips. Her arms extended up over her head, and she could not keep the wide grin from taking over.

Her smile of contentment quickly faded as the realization of yesterday's events smacked her in the face. Jerking to a quick upright position, she ran her hands through her hair. Her thoughts flashed back across the night. Everything had gone well, better than expected thanks to Alejandro.

Oh! Alejandro. Her knight in black leather on a Harley. He had carried the night. His bartending skills were artistic, his charisma like a beacon to the customers. Her head hit the pillow as she flopped backwards. She had pulled it off. Could she do it every day?

What do I do first?

Bringing her body up, she stretched.

Charles had greeted her every morning with a list of her daily duties. Most were routine, since she worked best with organization, they were easy.

But what about his duties?

Sitting crossed legged in the bed, she reflected.

What the hell did he do? Besides order her around and float through the café as the owner and big shot.

She swung her legs off the bed, her feet hitting the cool tile floor. Standing up, she grinned and stretched her arms over her head. Her mind told her to panic. She had the weight of the world on her shoulders, well at least her world. However, her heart told her she was to take one step at a time.

Her sweat pants lay over a chair. She slipped them on over her pj shorts, then picked up a denim shirt to throw over her tank top. Barefoot, she padded across the small apartment. Really, it was two apartments with one shared bathroom. While not fancy, it had given her a comfortable feeling from the first time she saw it. Large windows produced a spectacular view of the sea. Furnished with just a bed and dresser at one end, a table and love seat at the other, there were no decorations or personal touches in the living space. Still it was inviting and pleasant every time she entered.

Simple. It was simple and had been the one thing she had wanted most when they came to Italy. A simple life, working together to build a small but lucrative business.

The vast bathroom included a large tiled shower, a bathtub big enough for two, a porcelain sink, a walk-in closet and room to dance in the middle. Splashing refreshing cold water on her face, she looked at her reflection in the mirror.

Day one, girl!

Grabbing a towel, she wiped the water out of her eyes. Finishing her morning habit with brushing her teeth, she headed downstairs. The cool sea breeze touched her cheeks as she passed the open windows to the apartment door. This is what she had dreamed of, mornings full of sunlight and the smell of saltwater.

The café's kitchen was immaculate. Her first stop the coffee pot, she filled the water tank and scooped a rich dark Italian coffee into the filter. As it brewed, she leaned against the stainless steel counter and evaluated her options. She knew how to prep the food, arrange the dining room and have the staff ready for the dinner hour.

The cook, Benardo, came in at two o'clock. He was a bitter little man whose cruel remarks constantly upset the kitchen team. The staff was highly qualified, but they hated working for him.

Charles hired him. Imagine that.

Her mind wandered to speculate about what had led to Charles' departure.

Haven't a clue. Been too busy working, and moving and learning a new language to be aware of Charles' mid-life crisis.

She heard the beep signaling her coffee was ready. Pouring a cup, she cocked her head. *His mid-life crisis?*

What was all this follow your bliss about if not his mid-life crisis?

Her first cup of the day was always drunk while seated at the stainless steel prep table in the middle of the kitchen. The legs of the heavy metal stool grated along the ceramic floor as she pulled it out from under the table. She hopped up, feeling the cool bottom rungs on her bare feet as she braced her legs against them.

Something was missing. Jessica looked around. Everything was in its place. Shiny pots and pans hung on racks suspended from the high ceiling. Cooking utensils were arranged on a metal rack on the wall over the huge double sinks.

Silence.

The absence of Charles' voice made the silence loud. Resting her elbows on the counter, she let the good feeling wash over her bringing a smile.

Yeah.

She sipped the rich dark coffee with a touch of Italian crème.

Silence is good. What is that song? "Every-body's talking at me."

There was no one to talk at her this morning. And if she did it right, maybe every morning.

The taste of the expensive coffee started her mind in first gear. Slipping off the stool, she went to the cabinets, opened a drawer to get a pad of paper and a pencil. Propping herself back on the stool, she started a 'to do' list. Her mind snapped to sharp mode, and she tackled her task with a clear plan. Stopping now and then to think, her plan for the day fell into place.

Done!

Jessica looked up at the large clock.

And it was only nine o'clock.

Pouring herself a fresh cup of coffee, she gathered her list, headed back up to the apartment. Walking straight into the bathroom, she laid her pad and cup down on the counter. Reaching into the shower, she turned on the water.

No.

17

She turned it off.

I want to jog first.

Every morning back home Jessica would run in Central Park before work. She hadn't even taken a walk in the small village since they'd moved here. Her thoughts went back to when they first looked at the building. As she stood outside of the café, she thought about how nice it would be to jog down by the sea wall.

Going to the closet, she dug in a box she hadn't unpacked yet. Emerging from the closet she clutched her ratty tee shirt, glow-in-the-dark shorts in one hand, her running shoes and socks in the other. There was more to her standard attire for running, but what she had would do for today.

Dressing quickly, she bounced down the stairs, pass the dining room and out the kitchen's back door. At the alley, she sprinted down the narrow passageway. Rounding the brightly painted salmon colored building, she paced her jogging until she reached the street.

Flowers of all colors surrounded the sun bleached stone wall bordering the sea. The crystal clear blue of the water was surpassed only by the clear azure of the sky. Smooth sand spread out from the rocks to the waves. Jessica kept her jogging tempo slow but steady, giving her time to look around.

As many times as she had run in Central Park, she'd never noticed the beauty around her. Not even the change of seasons. How could she have existed in a world of no color or no feeling of utopia? No, she was the villain. Never stopping long enough to enjoy it, to appreciate what had been waiting for her at the dawn of each morning.

That will stop today.

From this day on she would run every morning. This was her world now.

Stopping her jog, she walked with her hands on her hips. The back drop for the sea was the many different colored buildings forming a semi-circle along the sea wall. Jessica turned her body around and took in the lavishness of the place that now was her home.

Home. Yes, it's my home, and it's time to claim it as such.

With her arms spread out, leaning her head back she closed her eyes and twirled around like a windmill. Then, she let her arms wrap around her body in a self-hug. She stopped spinning and for a moment stood still, her eyes closed.

Opening them slowly, Jessica let the wonder she felt manifest itself in a wide smile. Being on her own was not going to be bad. Her walk back to the café was a peaceful, calm.

This will be how I start each day filling my spirit, making my soul content.

The unlocked back door pushed open easily.

Now for the shower.

Up the stairs she sauntered, like a star-crossed lover, she touched everything as she passed. Today the world opened up. Her anger for now was dormant.

Go find yourself, Charles baby. You and Bambi. I am good where I am.

In the bathroom, she picked up her cold cup of coffee. The cooled sip still carried the taste of a rich, deep blend.

Good enough.

Once again, she turned on the shower. This time she entered it and let the warm water refresh her mind and body.

Dressing in her usual long colorful skirt and a white, tailored, over-sized shirt, she slipped on a pair of sandals. Feeling well put together, she went down to the kitchen with her 'to do list' in her hand.

It was noon and she knew what needed to be done in the next five hours to prepare for the dinner crowd. Checking the large walk-in coolers, she make notes of the supplies she had on hand.

The slam of the back screen door followed the call "groceries" signaled the arrival of her fresh produce, meat and dairy products. The older delivery man always greeted her with a smile, while his eyes traveled down her body. The first time it happened, she couldn't decide if she should be insulted or flattered. She decided flattered and today she welcomed the look. Dirk, as he said his name was, stopped as he placed a load of crates on her prep counter.

"Signora? You look most beautiful today." His broken English delighted her.

Letting a wide smile overtake her face, she leaned on the counter in a flirty pose, looking at his eyes. "Why thank you."

Dirk looked around. "And where is the man, Charles?"

Jessica had to laugh because it struck her as funny. "Gone. The man Charles is gone. Permanently gone, as in never coming back."

Dirk winked at her. "You are much more pleasant than him."

Benardo, her cook, burst into the kitchen. A small man with weathered skin and a rough voice.

Fire flashed in Dirk's eyes. "He didn't be gone also?"

"No." Jessica walked around the counter took Dirk's arm to keep the two men apart.

The disagreements between the two could sometimes be heard clear to the sea wall, she was sure. Guiding him to her desk area, she gave him a check, then steered him towards the door.

Benardo's discontented mumbles echoed behind them. Dirk started to turn around but Jessica kept a firm grip on his arm, getting him out the door, pushing him to his truck.

As he climbed up into the cab he turned and looked down at her. "Charles being gone. Does it make you sad?"

Shading her eyes from the sun with her hand, she shook her head. "No, not really. It should, shouldn't it?"

Dirk perched in the truck's cab, smiled down at her. "No, I think it is a good thing. You look happy. Your face, it glows."

Jessica smacked the door of the truck twice. "Go. You have flattered me enough for today. Thank you."

The kitchen's back door shook as Benardo charged out. "You call these peppers? I spit on them. They are poor excuse for peppers."

The ire in Dirk showed in his face. "You wouldn't know a good pepper if it bites you in your skinny ass." He shook his fist at the cook. The rest of his rant snapped in sharp Italian.

"Go!" Jessica commanded Dirk. Turning quickly she grabbed Benardo by his forearms, shoving him backwards. As he was a lightweight, she got him through the door as the truck drove off.

"These are not quality vegetables, none of this." Throwing his arms around as if he had just witnessed the worse tragedy.

Jessica did her best to keep a straight face. "It's all we have. I am so sorry. Next time I will speak to him." She had said these same words every day for two weeks. They seemed to calm the Benardo's raving beast as he walked over to the sink.

Jessica stood in the middle of the kitchen, her body shaking.

Lord, help me!

Jessica went to her next work spot, the dining room in the front of the café. Every day she made sure it would function and be presentable at five o'clock, the magic hour.

A radio sat on the back counter of the bar. She turned it on, standing still, listening as vivid Italian music filled the room. She smiled, went about her business. The noise floating from the kitchen told her the staff was working. The rich smells of peppers, garlic and chicken swirled across the dining room and filled the space with an inviting aroma. The sun coming in the windows today illuminated the room in a soft glow.

An hour later, the kitchen buzzed with activity. The staff rushed to complete the orders Benardo shouted at them. His voice could rake on a saint's last nerve.

In amazement, Jessica watched them work like a finely tuned orchestra creating the most marvelous meals. Today she found she was nervous as they shouted quips back and forth, feeling it was all on her shoulders. Last night she had a partner, just her job to do, with no reason to think about any disaster taking place if she did not keep on top of things.

Letting the swinging door shut quietly, she looked around the dining room. Everything stood ready. Tables and chairs sat waiting for customers. Perky and fresh, red and white flowers in vases, filled the room with a sweet aroma.

One last check on the kitchen through the glass window in the door, to be sure they were on task. Even though the language was strange, the gestures and body movements told her things were fine.

Italians spoke loudly and quickly with lots of hand signals. At first she had thought they were all mad at each other, but soon learned the difference between anger and normal talking.

The roar of a cycle vibrated the floor beneath Jessica's feet. Looking towards the back door, she saw a blur of black and silver pass.

Alejandro.

Her body relaxed and she breathed in the air around her. With him here, she had the added assurance it would be a good night. Pushing against the metal door, she entered the kitchen. Trying oh so hard to look in control, she braced her arms on the work table to stop the shaking.

The sun behind him as he entered produced a smoky, mysterious outline. She watched as all eyes in the kitchen turned to view the Roman god. The uncontrolled talking stopped and the silence bounced off the brick walls.

In all her years, Jessica had never seen a man command a room like Alejandro. She had stood at hundreds of cocktail parties and sat at several board meetings when rich and powerful men made their grand entrances. None compared to the simple but elegant way her black knight strolled in. His eyes searched the room until they landed on her.

He approached her with a relaxed and effortless stride. The wicked smile spreading to his eyes captured her undivided attention.

"Signorina Jessica." His panther-like movements ignored his surroundings. His voice washed over her spirit, calming her fears.

It is going to be okay.

Drawing up her body with her confidence, she let a faint smile crease her lips. "Alejandro." His name rolled off her tongue.

He was now within her breathing space, and she could smell the leather of his vest. The white shirt contrasted with his dark rich skin. His penetrating eyes flickered with amusement.

"Here as requested."

Jessica licked her lower lips and clamped her teeth to keep from stuttering. Her jaw clenched tight. Relaxing her face muscles, she answered as professional as she could. "Good."

Seconds, seeming like hours, passed as Jessica, mesmerized by his magnetism, stood as still as an Italian statue.

Finally, Alejandro's voice released his hold on her. "I will get setup, per voi."

Unable to move, she shook her head, looking around at the group of people staring at her.

"I need to help him." No one moved. Her voice took on a commanding tone. "Come on people. We have things to do."

As if she had shouted 'Action' everyone went back to what they were doing before Alejandro entered.

Better.

Jessica smoothed back her hair catching drops of sweat on her fingers.

Damn but it's hot in here.

CHAPTER THREE

"Please come this way."

The middle-aged couple followed Jessica as she walked ahead, tapping the two menus against her hand. Business was good tonight. It had been steady with several new customers. A table by the window was available, so she stopped and allowed the man to pull the chair out for his wife, she assumed, but she shouldn't in this day and age. After the man was seated, Jessica nodded to the waiter to approach.

The sound of shouting and breaking glass from the kitchen put Jessica on a dead run towards the closed swinging door. The voices became louder as she got closer. One of the male kitchen staffers bumped into her as he exited the kitchen in a rush.

Jessica steadied him but he pulled away, shouting as he moved from her.

"He is crazy. Can't work in this...place." His broken English and fright made him switch to Italian.

Jessica couldn't understand the spew of words, but she could guess what they meant. Benardo was on a rampage; one of many. He seemed to be having at least one a day. Snapping her body into her firm boss mode, she slapped the metal door as she knocked it inward.

A glass crashed at her feet.

"Benardo." Her voice strong and loud. "Stop this. Now."

"No." The angry little man looked like a small version of Napoleon.

Unfazed, she put her hands on her hips, moving calmly towards the stupid little man who dared to defy her. "Excuse me."

Benardo rose up to his full stature, which was probably five foot two at best. "I am an artist. I must have people who obey me." Waving his arms and hands in the air.

Face to face with the cook, Jessica widened her eyes and stared him down. "You are a mean, bitter little man, and you have no people. You are fired."

Her words took him aback, but he recovered quickly. "You can't fire me. Only the man Charles can. He hired me."

That does it.

Jessica's finger poked Benardo's chest as she backed him up to the door.

"The man Charles is no longer here. I am the boss. And you will not work for me, throw your little temper tantrums, or be mean to a staff who's more than your equal."

At the screen door, Benardo stopped. He remained indignant. "You will be sorry, Signora. You cannot run this restaurant without the man Charles and the great chef Benardo."

With one last shove, she pushed him out the door. "Don't count on it."

The screen door slammed shut with Benardo on the other side. With a huff, he left. Jessica leaned her head against the door jam.

What if he's right?

Then she heard the clapping of hands behind her. Turning she saw the kitchen staff smiling and shouting words she didn't understand, but they sounded friendly. The young waiter who had been the object of Benardo's wrath, stood in the swinging doors. Behind him, Alejandro stood holding the door open. His look told her she had done right.

Summoning up her dignity, Jessica pressed through her staff to the dining room. They patted her back and said sweet-sounding words.

At the door, she put her hands on Alejandro's waist, pushed him backward behind the bar.

"Quit smiling at me. What am I going to do now? I don't have a cook." The spark in his eyes gave her the sense he had the answers.

He ran his hands down her arms. "I have an Uncle who cooks."

"Of course you do. How big of a family do you and Josh have? Never mind, not important."

Jessica looked around the restaurant. The patrons were enjoying their meals. Some looked up and winked at her. The noise from the kitchen could not have escaped them, but they had stayed.

Turning her eyes back to Alejandro. "Will you talk to him?"

His finger traced down her jaw to her chin. Lifting her face so she was looking at him, his eyes said 'trust me'.

"Si. He will come and work for you."

"How can you be so sure?"

The wiry grin on his face justified his words. "Because I will tell him it is a...good thing."

A good thing. Sure it is.

She needed to get back in the kitchen. As she released Alejandro, he let his finger trail along her neck, down her shoulder, over her arm, to her hand. His touch was sensual and unsettling all at the same time.

Whirling around, she took two steps, paused, then put her trembling hand on the swinging door. As she entered everyone started speaking at once. Some English, some Italian.

Reaching the prep table she raised her arms. "One at a time."

She searched the faces stopping at Hector, the brunt of Benardo's rage. "What happened, Hector?"

Hector's face turned a low red as he stared down at the floor. "He said I picked up the wrong plate, but I didn't." His head rose proudly to the group. "He was wrong. Confused."

A million voices chimed in. Losing control of the crowd, Jessica raised her arms.

"Quiet." Putting her finger on her lips. "Sh-h-h."

The multitude of voices fell quiet.

She turned to Fiorenza, a prep cook. "Can you finish cooking and get the rest of the meals ready to serve?"

Fiorenza's smile lit up her motherly face. "Si. I am not as good a cook, but most is done. We can finish." She nodded to the rest of the crowd. They all nodded in agreement.

Feeling a rush of satisfaction well up inside of her, Jessica clapped her hands. They were with her and she could do this.

"Okay folks, let's do this."

Hector came to her side and put his hand on her arm, to stop her when she turned to leave.

"Tomorrow? What about tomorrow? I am so sorry." His young face pleaded with her.

Her hand covered his, patting it. "I have it under control. Not your fault. Now get to work. I'm paying you by the hour."

Smiling at him, she saw the relief on his face.

As she entered the dining room, she noticed several people standing at the bar. Handing their tabs to Alejandro, he rang up the sales. One of the waiters, Tristan an older, very experienced restaurant worker, had seated several more tables. Josh was busy clearing the tables as fast as the people left.

A big sigh of relief filled Jessica's lungs. Tristan turned as she approached, handed her the menus. Her hand brushed his shoulder in an appreciative gesture. His smile and bow told her she had done right. The next couple stepped up.

"This way please."

* * *

Midnight finally came giving Jessica permission to officially close. She slowly shut the front door, then mechanically turned the lock. Pausing to reach over to shut off the neon lights hanging in the windows, her feelings of fatigue told her the second night had been more challenging than the first. Her work weary body turned to face the clean-up needing to be done to properly end the night.

The staff was amazing. The café's dining area was ready for the next day. All the tablecloths and napkins were set to go to the laundry service. Bare tables with chairs stacked upside down reflected against the newly mopped floor. Josh was carrying the water pail and mop back into the kitchen.

Her eyes traveled over to the bar. Alejandro was giving the rich wood a last wipe. The bottles of liquors stood in a straight row, labels turned forward like little soldiers awaiting their command. The small window of the swinging doors showed the hustle and bustle of her staff at work in the fully lit kitchen. Shrugging her exhausted shoulders, her hands on the back of her hips, she popped her neck. Jessica moved towards the kitchen passing by the bar. Alejandro met her at the end, stopping her with his hand on her upper arm.

"You did well today, Signorina. You make your staff feel...appreciated."

Biting her lower lip, she laid a hand on his chest.

Is he always so hot, temperature-wise?

She leaned into him, his hand moved to caress her back, his face against her hair.

Then she jerked straight back, taking on her business tone. "It was a decision I had to make."

A curious grin flashed across his face, his hand still firm on her back. "You are a woman who knows her own mind. I like that."

His liking thrilled her. She wished it didn't. Even so, his few words of approval were better than Charles' long, drawn out, phony speeches he made to impress.

"I need to get in the kitchen. Make sure everything's going okay."

One of his hands rested at her waist. The intensity of his look pounded her until she had to move away.

Sweat beads clung to her finger tips as she brushed her hair back. Wiping the moisture on her skirt with one hand, she pushed the kitchen door open with the other. She didn't dare look back. Afraid her face would betray her feelings, she took a breath and walked with self-control into the mass of workers.

The staff stopped and looked at her.

For a lack of words, she blurted out, "So, how it's going?"

Fiorenza nodded, looking around at the others. At the back door stood a larger-than-life man. Jessica had no idea who he was, but his face, hidden behind a soft, blond beard, looked kind. His eyes were a warm brown, and he presented a pleasant smile.

She sensed a movement behind her, a familiar touch on her back.

Speaking against her ear, Alejandro spoke softly. "Signorina Jessica. This is my Uncle Salvador. The greatest chef in all of Italy."

The large man nodded, winked at Alejandro.

Jessica regained her composure. "And what makes him the best?"

While speaking, she turned her head towards Alejandro's face, only to find his lips a mini-speck from hers.

"He studied at the Le Cordon Bleu in Madrid." His sweet breath tickled her nose.

Turning back to look at the man, she narrowed her eyes. "Really?"

Salvador walked towards the couple. "Si. I have been Top Chef in some of the finest restaurants in all of Italy."

"So why do you want to work for my little café?" Jessica had her doubts.

This is too good to be true. I can't afford him.

She wanted him. In fact... "You're not Salvador Giordano?" Now closer to her, she recognized his face.

"Si, I am him." He raised both her hands, kissing them lightly.

Forgetting she was in a room full of people she turned to Alejandro. "I can't afford him." Her voice packed with panic.

The gentle giant cut in. "Excuse me Signora, but you can afford. Whatever you were paying the former chef, I take half."

Her look of disbelief swung from Alejandro to Salvador. "Half? Why would you take half?"

His features took on a faraway look. "As I said, I have worked at the best restaurants. I have made much money. But..." His eyes looked over at Alejandro. "I have fallen in love with a woman from this village."

Jessica was not getting the gist of this. Her eyes darted between Alejandro and his uncle.

The man continued. "We married and live here. We are having our first child."

Jessica was still skeptically. "Congratulations, but that does not explain why you are willing to work for me?"

His chuckle was pleasant and fatherly. "I must cook. I must cook for lots of people. It is in my soul. I can work for you, fulfill my desires and live peacefully with the woman I love. I would do it for free. Do you see?"

His story touched her heart. Drawing her hands up to her chest, she felt wetness in her eyes. "Oh, my. Yes, of course you can work for me, but not for free, or half. The going rate."

Turning, she winked at Alejandro, who looked over her head.

"Uncle Sal. It is the only amount she knows."

The staff in the kitchen cheered as they welcomed Salvador. A feeling of jubilation spread over her. Clapping her hands, she turned and threw herself into Alejandro's arms. His arms wrapped around her. His lips kissed her cheek. Feeling the comfort of his arms, she forgot they were boss and worker. He had saved her ass again, and she was ever so grateful.

Still holding her, Alejandro shouted to his uncle. "Welcome to our little family."

Our family. Echoed in her head.

Yes, this is beginning to feel like a family.

Each new addition was a splendid extra. Jessica pulled back slightly, not quite ready to leave the security of Alejandro's arms.

Her head turned to Salvador. "A drink. We need to make a toast to our future."

With Uncle Salvador on one side and Alejandro on the other, Jessica linked her arms through theirs. Together they filed into the bar area. She released her two men, Alejandro went behind the bar, Salvador led Jessica to a stool. When he lifted her up, she put her hands on his massive shoulders.

His caring, friendly eyes sparkled. He leaned against the bar. She could see the family resemblance between him and Alejandro.

"You are very lovely, Signora Jessica. And I can see good and passion in your eyes. Don't you see it, Alejandro?" He tilted back as Alejandro placed three shot glasses on the bar.

"Si." His voice drew her eyes away from the uncle to the nephew. "She is beautiful, and passionate. Yes, it is there." After pouring *Grappa* into three glasses, he set them up on the bar.

Each man picked up a glass, held it up and waited on her. Jessica picked up her glass, threw the crystal clear Italian liquor into her mouth. The searing, stinging liquid hit the back of her throat, burning all the way down to her stomach. Jessica hadn't done shots since college. The men followed suit.

Slamming the glasses on the bar, Alejandro and Sal watched her. Summoning up her best composure, she sat her glass down while feeling her eyes water.

Alejandro poured another round. Again the three of them clicked the glasses, downed the drinks.

With a big breath and nerves of steel, she knocked back the firewater as the Italians called it. Only this time it didn't burn so badly. Actually, she was feeling little pain. Slamming her glass down she dared him with her eyes to pour another one. His laugh was joined by Salvador's. Keeping his eyes locked with hers, he poured three more glasses without looking.

The three chugged the shots in unison. This time the liquid was soothing, calming. Jessica felt like she was floating. Male voices talked, yet they seemed so far away. The room swayed. Jessica grabbed the bar to keep from falling off the stool. Uncle Salvador steadied her, then she felt the strong arms of Alejandro around her waist.

In a fog, she heard them talking.

"Let's get her home." The deep baritone spoke. "Where does she live?"

"Upstairs." The sexy young voice said next to her ear. She leaned against him.

He feels so good.

"How do you know this, Alejandro?" The deep voice.

"I watch every night when she goes upstairs. I wait until the lights go out." The sexy voice.

Jessica rolled her head against the nice body. "That is so sweet." Her words were slurred. She knew some of her emotions were out there, but she didn't care. Today she had fired a small time cook and hired a world famous chef. She rocked.

Not quite passed out, she allowed Alejandro's strong arms to lift her. Her head nestled against his shoulders, her arms around his neck.

He smells delicious.

Up the stairs to her apartment, he carried her to the bed. The soft sheets and the cool sea breeze made her snuggle down in the bed. Alejandro removed the death grip she had on his neck and gently laid her arms across her chest.

His lips brushed her forehead. "Sleep, sweet lady."

She grabbed the front of his shirt. "We did good today. We are good together."

The warmth of his breath crossed her lips.

"Si. We are good together. Now sleep."

Letting go of him, she felt the darkness fold over her. Floating on a mist of pure contentment, she relaxed and let the feeling take over.

I did good, was her last thought.

CHAPTER FOUR

The pounding of a strong headache made Jessica bury her face under her pillow.

What the hell happened last night? Shots.

She had done shots with Alejandro and Uncle Sal.

Are you friggin' crazy?

Her memory recalled being carried up the stairs, the sweet smell of the neck she had burrowed her face in. Alejandro's face hovering over her as he laid her gently on the bed. She hoped she hadn't done or said anything stupid.

Like take me baby? No, there was another person in the room. Uncle Sal, my new cook. No chef. I think I was appropriate? Sure I was. I always am.

Removing the pillows carefully she peaked out from under the covers. Bright sunlight caused a blinding pain to shoot across her eyes. Ever so slowly she turned her head to look at the clock on the dresser.

Eight o'clock. Crap.

She needed to be up. She had a café to run.

When she eased out of the bed, turning away from the bright daylight, she staggered to the bathroom. Reaching in the cabinet, she grabbed the pain med's bottle.

Two, no three. This is a three pill headache.

The reflection in the mirror showed she still had her clothes on from the day before. *Crap.*

She needed a shower, but first she needed a cup of great strong Italian coffee. It was all the way down stairs in the kitchen. If she planned to survive her silly night of drinking, she needed the coffee to go with the shower.

Easing her way down the stairs, she clung to the wall for support.

When did they get so steep and so many of them?

At the bottom, she shielded her eyes from the day-light. Moving by instinct toward what she hoped was still the kitchen, she staggered. The closer she got the louder the music of an Italian opera beat against her brain.

Did I leave the radio on?

The overhead lights and the presence of a body as she entered the kitchen stopped her short. "Uncle Sal?"

The large man had vegetables, knives and pots all over the prep table. "Signora Jessica. You look a little pale? Are you...okay?" He walked over and steadied her with his hands on her arms, peering into her eyes. "Your eyes don't look so good."

"Yeah, well you should see them from my side." The heavenly smell of coffee made her turn around to the counter behind her. "Coffee."

Her intuition guided, as her brain was a bit slow. Pushing the wild mane of out-of-control hair from her face, she took a large cup off a hook, found her favorite cream next to the pot and poured the two together into the mug. The first sip was the best in the world as it crossed her lips and slipped down her dry throat.

Oh, but that hit the spot.

Maybe she would return to being human soon.

Gripping the cup with both hands, she straightened her shoulders and turned to see exactly what Sal was doing.

Why is he here so early? How did he get in? Did he take over? I am still the boss, aren't I? Who knows?

Leaning against the counter for support she took another sip and cleared her throat. "Why are you here so early? Benardo didn't come in until two o'clock."

Sal looked across his array of food at her. "Well, Benardo is no longer here. And for Salvador to do his best work, he starts early. Everything must be perfect."

No arguing with that.

"Well okay. I'm going to take a long shower since you seem to have everything under control."

Jessica walked around the table. Uncle Sal leaned down so she could kiss his cheek, his hands still busy chopping. "Thank you, Uncle Sal. You are a god send."

"And you, my dear lady, have given me a great gift, to be able to cook again for many people."

Going up the stairs was easier than coming down. Her step was lighter, her head clearer. The sea crashing on the rocks echoed hard off the walls of her apartment as she passed through to the bathroom. Stealing a quick glance at the unmade bed, it beckoned her to return to the quiet and comfort of sleep.

No, keep moving forward.

Entering the bathroom, she removed yesterday's clothes, tossing them in the hamper. She turned the shower on full blast, stepped into the steamy stream of hot water. Bracing her hands on the tile wall, she let the powerful flood of warm water flow over her head, down her back.

Better.

She was feeling almost normal again.

Today is going to be a good day.

* * *

The second trip down the stairs was welcomed more than the first. Jessica's walk was energetic, now she was ready to face the day. Finding Sal still in the kitchen working like an artist over his preparations, she noticed Dirk had left his daily order of fresh vegetables.

Speaking over her shoulder as she poured her second cup of coffee. "So you met Dirk?"

"Si. We have known each other for years. Good man. Good hard-working man. You like him?" Sal never stopped chopping, even when he talked.

A quick laugh escaped from Jessica. "Yes, I like him."

Things might get easier here now the cantankerous cook is gone.

Sal had convinced her he was a chef and Benardo had been just a cook.

Jessica had avoided the desk in the corner of the kitchen since Charles left. But now it was time to deal with the business side of owning the café. Gathering up her long skirt, she took the cup, with an imaginary suit of armor for protection, to the desk. She had organized it, so she knew where everything was and what it was.

Her desk chair welcomed her as she sat down, swirled toward the piles of papers and files. Starting with the one on top, she looked at it, sighed, then began her chore for the day. Her business needed to be kept together with organization and planning. The soft opera music and Sal's deep, rich voice singing along made background noise that soothed her into action.

* * *

Two hours later, leaning back to stretch, she was done. Everything was accounted for and prioritized. Not as bad as she expected, but then she handled the financial part of the business so she had a firm grip on the money. Even though they had saved and crunched the numbers, there were still expenses they hadn't expected. The outstanding balances needed to be dealt with in a timely matter.

Checking the bank statement on her computer, she was glad she hadn't made the bank deposit yet. If roving Charles tried to get any money out, there wasn't any. Since he had left all those "minor details" as he called them to her, all the accounts were in her name. Since she created them she could remove anyone at any time.

When the bank deposit was ready, she turned around in her chair to smell the most delightful aroma she had ever encountered. Sal motioned with his hand to a place set up at the end of the table, a bowl of steamy pasta at the center.

"Signora, come. You need lunch." A proud-papa smile played around his mouth.

Jessica's stomach growled as if saying, "Don't you dare refuse". She couldn't. Totally famished, she needed the enrichment the food offered. Curtsying to Sal, she then hopped up on the stool to survey the array of food in front of her. With the pasta was freshly baked bread, rich creamy butter and a spinach salad with strawberries, tomatoes and pecans. A wine glass held a translucent red liquid. Holding the glass in her hand, Jessica winked at Sal, then swirled it, making the wine move in a spiral motion. Raising it to her nose, she took a deep breath, closed her eyes, then sipped the cool, full bodied juice of the gods.

"Excellent." Her eyes opened to find Sal waiting with anticipation. His wide smile broke across his face, filling his eyes.

Setting down the glass, she picked up the fork, stabbed the awaiting salad. The mixture of fruits and vegetables was intensified by a sweet-sour dressing of raspberry and garlic flavored vinegars. She could not speak with her mouth full so she just nodded her head with approval. Sal's pleasure made his face light up. So pleased with himself, Jessica had to admit.

He is an artist.

Jessica motioned with her empty fork for him to join her. Sal pulled a stool under him, sat down, crossing his arms on the table.

"Damn, Uncle Sal. This is the best food, ever." Jessica couldn't wait to taste the pasta.

Shrimp, peppers and mushrooms drowned in a sumptuous cream sauce, smoothly flowed over her taste buds. Soft and crunchy, the blend of flavors woke up her senses. It almost felt like a sexual experience. Only sex never tasted this good.

Swallowing the superb cuisine, Jessica leaned back to take a break.

Okay, hiring Sal was a stroke of pure luck and fantastic foresight.

They talked together as she finished her lunch. Sal addressed her with such respect. She felt a deep friendship starting to form.

"Signora Jessica, you are very beautiful. Very intelligent. You will make a good boss. Alejandro says your husband left you. Not to pry, but he very stupid man."

Jessica rolled her lips together so she didn't spew her wine all over him. "I must agree. He is a stupid man."

"Then we will prove him stupid. We will have the best café in all of the village. No, all of Italy."

Covering his hand with hers, she smiled into the friendly eyes.

"All of the village is good enough. I am glad you and Alejandro work for me. You have made me believe in myself. A woman's self-esteem gets kicked pretty hard when she loses a husband."

"You not lose him. He lose you." A touch of anger sounded in his voice. "Beside you have Alejandro. He will be your man."

"Have you told this to Alejandro?" She had to grin at his remark as she dabbed her lips with the cloth napkin. Finished with her meal, Jessica slid off the chair.

Sal looked at her in surprise. "What's to tell? He would do anything for the lovely Signora Jessica."

Laying her hand on the side of his face, she let him know she was pleased. "With such strong, kind men, I will fear nothing. Thank you."

His large, warm hand covered hers, his head nodded.

Jessica was touch by the simple emotions the two exchanged. She grimaced, changing the subject so her emotions stayed in checked. "Now, I have to run some errands. It's noon, so I will only be gone for an hour or so. Need anything?"

"I have all I need." Sal replied. "Go enjoy the day."

Over at her desk she gathered up her bank bag and some letters to mail. She was looking forward to the nice walk after such a filling meal. The day had stayed sunny, she was glad. Her head returned back to normal, her brain no longer fuzzy. She took in a deep breath when she stepped out the back door. With a spring in her step, she followed the narrow roadway to the business part of the village.

* * *

The woman at the bank recognized Jessica as she stepped up to the window. "Signora Anderson."

Jessica acknowledged the teller with a smile as she pulled her money and papers out of her bag, laid them in order on the counter. The woman did each transaction with precise attention. When she had finished, she pushed the receipts towards Jessica.

"Anything else, Signora?"

"Yes." It was giving her great pleasure to say this, "Please remove my husband's name from all of the accounts. He is no longer part of the business." She tapped her fingertips on the counter.

The teller punched the keys on her computer. Looking at the screen, she repeated Jessica's instructions back to her. "Remove Charles Anderson from the accounts." With a flare, she hit the last key, turned to Jessica with a smile. "Done."

"That easy?" Jessica kind of wanted a little more pomp to bring her closure and satisfaction.

"That's it. Doesn't take much to remove them from a bank account. It does take a lot more to remove them from your life."

Jessica chuckled. "Not always. Have a good day." She swung around, nodding to the little Italian lady behind her. Pushing the heavy glass doors open, she stepped outside.

Now, that's done. I am freeing myself one step at a time.

The warm Italian day swept over her, her spirit soared. She knew she was going to be free in this beautiful country to live as she wanted.

Just about to step off the curb, she was stopped by a large Harley pulling up in front of her. The smile inside the helmet was quickly recognized.

Alejandro.

She put her hand on his shoulder to keep from falling on him. He looked up at the bank's sign.

"Are you robbing it? Need a get-away driver?" His mischievous smile danced around his eyes.

Resting her hand casually on his shoulder, her mood was just right for a little fun banter. "You would be my man if I needed one."

The dazzling smile tweaking his lips made her think how very handsome he was.

"So hop on Signorina Jessica, I will take you far, far away. They will never catch you."

Tossing her hair back, she thought for just a moment what it would be like to go far, far away with him. However, logic brought her back to her senses. Her laugh was real. For she was jovial and he was handsome.

"Another time. We will run away together another time."

"So for now, hop on. I'll take you back." He handed her a helmet.

She took the helmet in both hands, looked at him. "What?"

He stood up, balanced the bike between his thighs and patted the second seat behind him. "Come on, it's safe. I'm good at this."

Jessica looked down at the helmet, shrugged. She gathered up her hair, pushed into helmet. As she started to swing her leg over the seat, she became entangled in her long skirt.

"Pull it between your legs." Alejandro instructed her.

She gave him a sharp look. "I beg your pardon?"

His laugh mocked her. "Your skirt. Pull it between your legs, tuck it in your waistband, then swing on."

Embarrassed, she did as he said. Holding on to his strong shoulders she climbed on behind him. Her butt formed to the leather, warm against her skin even through the skirt's material.

Alejandro's voice instructed her. "Grab hold of my waist and hang on."

The cycle jumped slightly as he gunned the motor, lifted his feet. Jessica held on to him so tightly she could feel his muscles against her chest. Their bodies intimately formed together.

The wind whipped across the unprotected area of her face. The bike weaved in and out of the traffic. She knew she should be scared, but she felt such freedom. She laid her chin on his shoulder, her cheek resting against the smoothness of his face.

The beauty of the village passed by quickly, but the blur only added to the excitement. She could get used to this. Alejandro had brought a new element to her life. Expecting to live a quiet, simple life, instead she flew down cobblestone streets behind a young stud. People on the street waved. This was definitely his village.

CHAPTER FIVE

The exhilarating bike ride ended all too soon. Rounding the building, Alejandro reduced the bike's speed, putting one foot down to steady it. Jessica followed the direction of his body in the turn. When they were at a complete stop, she leaned her head against his back, daydreaming of flying away forever after the invigorating ride.

Alejandro's sexy voice cut through her thoughts. "Signorina Jessica?"

Softly, she purred. "Si."

"Are you going to get off?" His voice flowed over her like a cool waterfall.

When the understanding grasped her, she jerked upright. "Yes, of course. We're here?"

Her hands grabbed his shoulders as she tried to dismount gracefully. However, her long skirt caught on the bike. She tugged and tugged but it didn't budge. Alejandro twisted around to look at her, as if wanting to know what the holdup was.

Feeling awkward, she tried to explain. "I'm stuck. I mean my skirt is." She tugged on it again. "Can you help, please?"

Turning around to the other side, he reached down to free her skirt. The hem drifted over the seat, fell down to her feet. She gathered it up, stepping back. The mid-day heat made her hair tumble down in her eyes. Pushing it back, she gave him a weak smile and turned toward the back door.

Stopping suddenly, she turned back. "Thank you for the ride." Clutching the bank bag to her chest, she felt like a high school girl thanking the cool boy for carrying her books.

Alejandro nodded. "Anytime, Signorina." He scooted his bike over by the trash bin, dismounted like a cowboy from a proud stallion.

Jessica wanted to go into the building, but instead she stood transfixed, watching him. The opening of the screen door snapped her out of her trance. Josh grabbed her arm. "Signora Jessica, customers are lining up already." His voice carried a hint of panic.

"What? Why?" A glance at her watch told her it was just four o'clock.

Josh pulled her inside, the kitchen staff was buzzing with words and actions. Allowing him to pull her into the dining room, she saw a line of people in front of her windows. Tristan had many of the tables set up, Josh rushed over to help him.

Alejandro had followed them in and was tying his apron on. He walked over to her, putting her apron over her head.

Reaching behind her, he wrapped the string around, back to the front tying it as he pulled her close. His breath hot on her chest.

When he was done he turned her towards the front of the café, shoving her lightly. "Go."

Jessica obeyed, and went to the hostess' stand. She checked to make sure everything was in its proper place. Giving the room a final check, she rushed to the kitchen. "What is going on? Why are they all here now?"

Fiorenza patted Jessica's shoulder. "Word spreads fast Salvador is the new chef. Everyone wants to eat his cooking."

Jessica looked around at the staff, settling her gaze on Sal.

He shrugged. "Well, maybe I tell a few friends."

Panic creased her face. "Do we have enough food, people...Oh crap? Servers? There's only Tristan."

Fine. Charles not only left me without a bartender, he took Bambi. Not that she was any good as a waitress.

Jessica hadn't bothered to replace the bimbo as they seemed to be handling the customers fine, but now...

Sal's rumbling voice cut through her torrent of thoughts. "We will be good. Alejandro, call Roberto and Fernando. They will come."

Jessica had not heard Alejandro behind her.

"Si, Uncle Sal." He flipped open his cell, walked away talking into the phone.

Jessica's eyes swept the kitchen, the faces staring back at her were calm and smiling.

They're ready for this. So you get ready, girl. You're running a business.

* * *

Roberto and Fernando arrived within fifteen minutes. Jessica had come into the kitchen to grab a bite to eat when the duo entered.

They had to be cousins, because they looked as good, uh, just like Alejandro.

Tristan greeted them, shouting in Italian and shaking their hands. His explanations were also spoken in Italian. The cousins immediately took their directions, putting on aprons they went out into the dining room. Jessica stood speechless as the staff took over her café.

By four-thirty everyone was in place. Jessica, at her hostess stand, looked around again, impressed with the professional way her staff worked.

Alejandro came strolling over to her. "Signorina Jessica, this is Fernando."

The young, handsome man took her hand, kissing it lightly. Raising his head, his smile was charming, adorable. "Signorina, it is a pleasure."

Jessica looked over his head at Alejandro. "Really?"

Alejandro returned his devious smile and nodded. Fernando released her hand to step back.

Moving in-between, with a quick motion Roberto grabbed her hand. "Also my pleasure." His kiss on her hand tingled her skin. His eyes flickered with temptation. His smile was sinfully sexy and left the impression he was ready for anything. Anything. Jessica rolled her lips to keep from laughing.

This one I'll watch.

She raised her gaze back to Alejandro. His look let her know she was right. That cousin was a player.

When Roberto lifted his head, she pulled her hand back. "Welcome boys and thanks for being willing to help out. You're saving my..." Looking up, meeting Alejandro's grin she stopped "...café."

Roberto clapped his hands. "Okay, let's rock and roll. Open those doors. We are ready."

Feeling giddy, Jessica grabbed a handful of menus and marched to the door. Flipping the switch, the open sign fluttered then shone brightly. The customers in line turned towards the door, closed rank, then stood patiently.

Jessica took the first four patrons to a table, brushing arms as she passed by Alejandro escorting the second six to another table. The clockwork way in which they seated all the people the café could hold made Jessica feel confident. Even with the dining room full, the line outside was snaking down the sidewalk and out of sight.

The crowd never let up. At midnight the café was still full. Jessica leaned on her stand, tired, hungry, but ecstatic. Several of the customers had made a point to give the chef their compliments. Most knew of Salvador Giordano. His reputation preceded him. Those who had experienced the chef's mastery for the first time left satisfied, promising to return.

Seeing a break in the crowd, Jessica slipped into the kitchen. Spotting her chef at the stove, stirring a rich red sauce that steamed up the bricks, she walked over to him.

"Sal, where is all the food coming from? Do we have enough? I need to order more for tomorrow. Will this happen again tomorrow?" Her words came in a flood, and she knew she was rambling.

Sal stopped his cooking to take her hands. "I have everything under control. Is it not good you have business?"

Jessica stopped speaking and gripped his hands.

"You are pleased, no?" Sal frowned.

Jessica nodded.

His deep laugh echoed. "Then let me run the kitchen."

Her voice strained, she asked too quietly for anyone else to hear. "Okay, but are we ready for this?"

Her questions were greeted with a pleasant smile. Kissing both of her hands, his beard tickled her skin. When he released them, they fell limp to her side.

"Signora Jessica, I have already ordered what we will need from Dirk." Sal turned back to stir his sauce. "I would have been surprised if this had not happened."

Jessica wrapped her arms around Sal's waist, hugging him. She felt his back vibrate with his chuckle. Letting go, she patted his back, then twirled around bumping into Roberto.

His hands went suggestively to her waist, pulling her slightly into him. His eyes rested on her bust. "You are a success. Let's celebrate."

There was no mistaking his intentions, but Jessica had no desire to participate. "I celebrated last night."

A small chuckle from Sal sounded behind her. Prying herself from Roberto's grip, she pushed him aside.

Jessica went back to the dining room, pausing at the door to look over at Alejandro. Before she thought, she walked over to him, laid her hand on his arm. He stopped what he was doing and turned to her. His eyes twinkled with the same welcoming look they always had when they looked at her.

Her words seemed hollow, but she didn't know what else to say to thank him for helping her so much. "Thank you." Going up on her tiptoes, she kissed his cheek. His familiar sweet smell rose to greet her. The memory of him carrying her last night touched her mind softly.

His hand steadied her. "You are more than welcome. It is all good, si?"

"Si."

The comforting feeling he radiated felt different than any she had known. It was his belief in her and the support she needed to keep her head held high. Dislodging herself, she backed away from him. At the end of the bar she turned to walk to her station. Pushing her hair from her face, she suddenly felt like a woman coming into her own.

* * *

It was well passed two o'clock in the morning when Jessica finally turned the key on the front door and switched off the 'open' light. This had been the longest day. She leaned her back against the closed door. Again, her staff had the night cleaning done. The dining room ready to start again tomorrow. The three waiters stood over by the bar talking and joking with Alejandro.

Such a handsome group. Are all Italian men drop-dead gorgeous?

Sal came through the kitchen door, heading for her with out-stretched arms. Pushing herself from the door, she stumbled to him. His bear hug nearly choked the breath out of her.

"Signora Jessica. You have made me very happy." His deep baritone sounded like he was singing. "It has been months since I cooked for such a willing crowd. Tomorrow night will be better."

Jessica drew back and looked at him. "Better? You mean more customers?" Her mind doubted her ability to meet the demands of more people.

Sal wrinkled his brow to look at her. "You not want a successful café?

The desire to succeed flashed up her body and caught fire in her soul.

Yes, I want to pull this off. Especially since Charles walked out thinking he left me to fall flat on my ass.

Squaring her shoulders, she took Sal's face in her hands. "Yes, I want all the business I can get. Bring it on. We..."She looked around at the waiters who had gathered around them. Her eyes rested on Alejandro. "... can handle it." His smile reflected her positive feeling.

Roberto wrapped his arms around her shoulders. "I say we celebrate." His lips spoke against her neck. "Come with us pretty lady. I will show you the time of your life." The warmth of his breath brought goose bumps to her arms.

Untangling herself, she slipped over by Alejandro seeking protection. "Not tonight boys. I am still recovering from last night."

Alejandro lightly touched her waist. "Go upstairs, Signorina Jessica. Sleep well. Dream good."

Moving slowly out of his touch she nodded to the rest, then turned to ascend the stairs, knowing she was being watched. Once inside the door, she could hear the voices of the men bidding goodnight to each other. The sound of the voices fading told her they exited out the back door, leaving only the quiet which meant she was alone.

For some reason, being by herself did not frightened her as she had expected. Once In the bathroom, she changed her clothes and brushed her teeth. Going back out to her bed, she pulled back the covers. Fragments of the conversation from the night before seeped back into her memory. Her head had been foggy but the words still floated through her liquor-soaked brain to stay with her. Now they surfaced.

"Let's get her home." The deep baritone spoke. "Where does she live?"

"Upstairs." The sexy young voice.

"How do you know this, Alejandro?" The deep voice.

"I watch every night as she goes upstairs. I wait until the lights go out." The sexy voice.

Jessica looked over at the double French doors leading to her small, but very own terrace. She had only walked outside once, the first time she had seen the apartment. The view of the sea had been breathtaking. She could see the whole village to the outskirts. Standing there, she imagined morning cups of coffee and end-of-the-day glasses of wine.

As if compelled by an unseen force, she moved to the doors. She slowly unlatched them, shoving them open with ease. At the railing, she looked down at the street-light illuminating a space in the darkness. A fresh fog rolled in from the sea, circling the person under the glow. A dark figure sat on a shiny Harley, a helmet hanging on the handle bars. His face turned up towards her.

Alejandro.

He sat like a sentinel guarding a most valuable prize. His look did not waiver from her.

Raising her hand, she waved to him. He answered back with a nod. For several moments they stared at each other. His presence soothed her. She felt she was not without reinforcements, for the universe had sent her some of the most awesome helping hands, starting with Alejandro. His name echoed through her mind like a familiar song. With it came warmth, tenderness and kindness.

Was it really only three days ago I thought my world was crashing down?

Now her strength had been renewed by a group of kind people who somehow were all related.

The damp night air chilled her. Rubbing her bare arms, she signaled with her hand she was going back in. Even this far away she could see his dazzling smile. Again he nodded.

Reluctantly, she turned away from the vision in the mist to go back to the warmth of her apartment. Shutting the double doors, she leaned her head against the frame as she locked them. She flipped off the light switch. The room went dark except for the moonlight's gleam infiltrating the haze of the sea air.

Slipping into her comfortable bed, she heard the soft roar of the motorcycle as it faded into the distance.

Yes, I have a knight in shining armor looking out for me.

The coziness of the thought surrounded her, luring her into a peaceful sleep.

CHAPTER SIX

"Jessica!" the shrill female voice made Jessica turn away from Alejandro to seek the annoying sound. In fact, the whole restaurant turned to see from whom the sound was coming. A stylish woman in a champagne Chanel pantsuit stood in the doorway, holding her Chanel sunglasses in her manicured hand, a Chanel purse slung over her shoulder. With her immaculate hair, make-up and body, she stood like a celebrity greeting her public. Jessica let a smile spread across her face as she left the bar to greet her longtime friend, Carly.

"Well, look here." Jessica opened out her arms as she flew across the room.

The two women hugged, jumping up and down as they squealed.

Carly held Jessica at arm's length, her voice heavy with a phony, non-descript accent. "You look marvelous, darling!"

Jessica linked her arm through Carly's. "Come, there is someone I want you to meet."

Walking towards the bar, Carly ran her finger along the top of the checkered table cloths.

"Quaint, charming, sweet." Her voice dripped with deceptive compliments.

Jessica was aware of Carly looking around the room. As they approached the bar, Alejandro reached up to remove one of the hanging glasses from a rack, his firm body stretching. Fixing his eyes on the women, his face broke into his charming, sexy smile.

Carly lowered her sunglasses to look over them. "And what do we have here? Oh, my." Carly pried her body from Jessica's relaxed hold. Jessica sat up on the bar stool.

"Carly. Alejandro." Jessica waved her hand as she acknowledged each of them.

"Oh my, you are gorgeous." Carly's voice was low and seductive. Jessica tilted her head to see if drool actually was flowing down her friend's chin.

Alejandro kissed Carly's hand, "Welcome to *Di Me Sogni*. The staff and I welcome you."

"Do they all look like you?" Carly's voice was barely a whisper.

Alejandro nodded his head towards the waiter's station. Her eyes followed his direction.

Scrutinizing the rest of the men, she said. "Jessica, do you know you have a stable of studs working here?"

Jessica chuckled. "They're my staff. They saved my ass when Charles walked out."

Carly's head snapped around. "Charles walked out?"

"Yeah, couldn't take the pressure. Went off with a young, cheap waitress. Left me with all this." Jessica gestured around the room with her arm. "So I hired Alejandro. And he helped by bringing his friends-slash-family to work. They're good."

Carly took Jessica's hands and held them tight. "Are you all right? Oh my god, I'm so sorry."

"As good as I can be. I have the business to keep me focused, grounded."

Placing her hand on the edge of the bar, Carly gave Jessica her full attention. "Are you making it here?"

Jessica shrugged. "Sort of." She looked her friend in the eyes, couldn't lie. "Barely. Things have picked up since I hired this magnificent chef. But I have a ways to go before I am in the money, so to speak."

Carly turned and put her back against the bar, her elbows on either side of her. She looked around at the customers, then over at the staff. Jessica could tell she was thinking up an idea.

They had worked together in New York at a top fashion house. Carly's stylishness, whether designing a fashion show or a showroom, propelled her to the top of the company. Jessica had a head for marketing. Together they had orchestrated some unique and impressive deals.

"What are you thinking?" Jessica's words brought Carly out of a trance-like state. Jessica had seen her work wonders with a scheme.

Carly's face beamed. "How about I try some of your food, and we'll discuss this." She linked her arm through Jessica's and pulled her from the stool. "Have I got a plan for you."

Together the two women slipped into the kitchen.

Sal was leaning over the stove, but he straightened up when he heard them. "Signora, who is this vision of womanhood beside you?"

Jessica heard Carly giggle.

"I love Italian men when they talk like that." Carly whispered to Jessica.

Jessica laughed. "Uncle Sal, this is my best friend, Carly."

Carly untangled herself from Jessica, sauntered over to the large man.

"Uncle Sal." Her words rolled off her tongue with a slight accent. His hand released the ladle and bowing, he lowered his lips to her raised hand.

"And lovely lady, what brings you to our humble establishment?"

Carly let her hand remain in Sal's. "The word is out. The great Salvador was cooking at this small, but impressive café on the shores of the Mediterranean. I had to come and see. Lo and behold it was at my friend's place that he resides." She bowed to him.

Sal's face lit up, his smile creased his eyes. "Then I must create an elite dish for the friend of a most special lady in my life. Please allow me some time to create not only a culinary masterpiece, but also an atmosphere to enjoy the view of the charming village that is my home. Signora Jessica, if you would please take a stroll along our lovely beach with your dear friend and give me some creative leeway, I will do you proud."

The laughter rolled from Jessica's throat. "Uncle Sal, you always do me proud. But the customers?"

"Will be in good hands." Uncle Sal's tone commanding. "Please give me some space and time." He clapped his hand together in front of his chest and shook them.

Jessica was touched by his insistence.

"Okay, as per your wishes, we will take a stroll along the white sands of our lovely beach."

Sal released Carly's hand and gave her a light push towards Jessica. Linking their arms, the two women stepped out into the fading sunlight of dusk. In spite of the setting sun, the balmy air enveloped them as they strolled down the stone streets of the village.

* * *

"So tell me..."Carly started the conversation as they walked along the sea wall. "...what happened between you and Charles?"

Jessica squeezed Carly's arm. "I honestly thought I didn't know at the time. Jessica shook her head. "I know all women say that when their husbands cheat. But I didn't see this coming."

Carly returned Jessica's arm hug. "I always thought he was a rather pompous little ass. So he cheated on you? No warning?"

Jessica let go of Carly to lean on the edge of the wall. The rough rocks pierced her hands. The waves rolled to the shore with a peaceful grace. The calm sea helped Jessica think deeply about what Carly was asking.

"Maybe I was too focused on getting to our goal to notice one of us was going in a different direction." The admission made Jessica think back. Looking over at Carly, she finally saw the clear picture of what had been so fuzzy.

"I was so excited about selling it all and moving to Italy. Our marriage was rocky, dormant after ten years. We took a vacation to renew our love. When we came to this village, a plan formed." Jessica looked down at her feet, leaning forward. "The fast track had been our life. The desire to live the simple and quiet life in this village was like a burning ember." Clutching her fist to her chest, she thought of how the fire started as a spark then grew to a strong purpose. Having it yanked away by a cheating husband was not a thought she had entertained. "I wanted to have kids." The statement hurt, and she wrapped her arms around her waist.

Carly put her arms around Jessica's shoulder. "I envy you. Being courageous enough to make all of this happen."

The snicker came out before Jessica could stop it.

"Courageous? How much courage does it take to have blinders on and see nothing going on around you? Thinking only of your own needs and wants?" Shifting her weight, Jessica turned to her dear friend. "I guess I could have paid more attention, but I was determined to get us here. And we got here, just somewhere along the line I lost a husband."

The café was just a few feet away from where they sat.

Getting to her feet, Jessica took Carly's hand. "Enough! Let's see what magnificent meal Sal has made for us."

Giggling like school girls, they crossed the street dodging cars and people. The front door opened as she reached for the knob. Josh stood back as they entered.

"Ladies. Please follow me to your dining spot."

Jessica looked around at the full dining room. "This is the dining area."

"No, a special place has been reserved for your eating pleasure tonight. Please?" Josh gestured with his hand for them to follow his lead. Both women looked at each other and shrugged.

As they passed the bar, Alejandro was making a drink, but he turned and winked at Jessica. She smiled, shrugged her shoulders to say what's going on, he just returned her smile. Turning around quickly, she bumped into Josh, who had stopped walking. They were at the bottom of the stairs to her apartment.

"Up there?"

Josh nodded his answer.

Carly looked up the stairs. "What's up there?"

Jessica kept her eyes on Josh. "Where I live."

"Oh, let's go." Carly took the steps two at a time.

Jessica shot Josh a look, suspicious of all of this. Looking back at Alejandro, she saw him leaning on the bar watching. His eyes flashed a 'trust me' look. Her skirt brushed against Josh's leg as she started up.

What's waiting for me to see?

The men in her life, Alejandro, Josh, Uncle Sal, Roberto and Fernando were always full of surprises. Good surprises, but unexpected actions, nevertheless. In less than a month, Jessica felt as if she had inherited two brothers, a cousin, a kind uncle and Alejandro. Everyone brought something to the table. Some more than others.

By the time Jessica and Josh had reached the apartment, Carly had taken her own private tour. "What a delightful place. Wonderful, pleasant...simple."

Looking around, Jessica whispered to Josh, "Where's the food?"

Josh's smile almost mimicked Alejandro. He crossed the small seating area, opened the double

French doors to the loggia. Jessica followed him as he went outside.

The area was surrounded by twinkling lights casting a faint glow over the flower-covered banister. Candles of all sizes were lit and scattered around the small space. Classical Italian music faintly rode on the warm night air. A table just big enough for two was set with Vietri Incanto Baroque china and Waterford crystal glasses on a jet black tablecloth.

Jessica slipped her arm through Josh's. "This is so lovely, so magical." She leaned her head on his shoulder. "Thank you."

Josh's arm relaxed. "So you are pleased?"

Squeezing his arm, Jessica replied. "Yes, I am very..."

The sharp voice of Carly cut off her last words. "Oh my gawd! This is absolutely fantastic. Jessica, you live in a dreamland."

Jessica moved away from Josh. "It does seem like that at times."

Shifting with the grace of a well-trained maître de, Josh pulled out a chair for Carly and then for Jessica. Each sat, allowing Josh to put the cloth napkins in their laps. The display on the table was breathtaking. A center piece of white gardenias and black candles accented the white china. Josh poured a light amber sparkling wine into first Carly's glass and then into Jessica's.

The women clinked their glasses.

The reflection of the candles sparkled in Carly's eyes as she presented a toast. "To you my dear friend. You are a strong, sharp lady who will survive this... injustice."

Jessica leaned forward as she laughed. "And to you my dear friend who always seems to know when I need her and comes to my rescue."

Josh appeared with chilled plates of a spinach and mushroom salad tossed with a rich garlic asiago dressing topped with toasted bread cubes.

"To die for!" Carly's high pitched voice paired with the wave of her fork.

Her mouth full of food, Jessica just nodded.

Yes, to die for.

* * *

In the afterglow of a satisfying seven course meal, Jessica leaned back, throwing her arm over the back of the chair. The night sky was clear. The stars felt so close their brightness seemed to touch the corner of the sea.

This was one of those times in life that... what was the saying, 'It doesn't get any better than this'.

The rustle of jeans turned Jessica's attention to the door as her three main men walked into her enchanted space. Roberto led the entourage, swaggering in with his girl-killer smile.

"Lovely ladies." His heavily accented voice was seductive. "We would like to take you to a lively and..." He leaned around Carly's chair and spoke against her neck "very hip dance club to boogie the night away."

Jessica's gaze switched from face to face. "The café? Is it...?" Her watch showed her it was twelve forty-five p.m. "...closed?"

Alejandro leaned his amazing form against the railing, arms folded across his chest. "Everything is done. Uncle Sal will close up. You my beautiful lady need a night on the town."

In one quick motion he moved to her, pulling her to her feet. Encircling her waist, he moved his body against her in a seductive sway. He spoke against her hair. "You need to feel the music, the magic of Italy."

Jessica moved with him for a moment, before the reality of what she was doing engulfed her. Easily, she moved back, smoothed the front of her skirt down, pushed her hair back.

Tearing her eyes from Alejandro's handsome face, Jessica turned to look at Carly. "Carly, what do you say?" Roberto and Carly sat close together, talking and smiling in an intimate way.

In a seductive voice, Carly answered Jessica's question. "Carly says yes. Let's go."

Jessica hesitated, looking back at Alejandro. The smiling eyes beckoned her. Her resolve melted.

Why not.

"I suppose we are going on your bike?" She smiled.

Go with the flow.

He shrugged, tilted his head.

"Fine. I'm changing. The last time I rode your bike wearing a skirt was... well... the last time I ride your bike in a skirt."

Everyone followed Jessica as she walked back inside. "I'll meet you down-stairs." She tossed back over her shoulder as she headed for the bathroom. The rest of the group trooped down the stairway. Jessica grabbed a pair of jeans out of her closet and changed. Looking in the mirror, she brushed and fluffed her hair.

Yeah, a night out will do me good.

Carly had brought some fun back into her life, even if it was just for a little while.

Her step had a bounce as she skipped down the stairs, through the kitchen and out the back door. Alejandro was sitting on his bike, the machine vibrating lightly. As he handed her a helmet, she smiled at him. She put on the helmet, then swung her legs over the back seat and wrapped her arms around his waist.

Carly was behind Roberto. The contrast of the black jean clad handsome man and the sharply dressed woman looked natural. Fernando rode alone. Jessica smiled over at him. He was more reserved than his brother, but just as appealing.

Alejandro kicked up his stand, gunned his motor making the bike lurch forward. Leading the pack from the dark alley, to the subdued light of the cobblestone streets, and on to the bright lights of the city beyond.

Jessica felt the warmth of his skin through his shirt. The smell of his neck was a mixture of musk soap and Polo cologne. The night air lingered with the day's warmth. Jessica leaned her chin on his shoulder. Watching the world come at her at a high speed, so open, so there, was bringing a new joie de vivre. She had never ridden a motorcycle at night before.

It had been a long time since she felt this young and free. Her life had always mostly been planned. When a plan fell apart, she had no idea what she should do besides keeping to the schedule.

But when do you go to plan B?

Alejandro guided the bike to the parking area, brought it to a stop and cut the motor. While he balanced the bike, Jessica dismounted. Standing next to him as he put the kickstand down, she admired the agile movement of his body as he swung his leg over. As he stood in front of her, his heat radiated to her. Wrapping his arms over her shoulders, he turned her towards the dance club's door. When they caught up with the other three, Jessica linked one of her arms through Fernando's.

"Let's do this, boys. Teach me how to party Italian style."

CHAPTER SEVEN

A leg touched Jessica's thighs. Her mind came awake with a jolt of "OMG" reality.

Who is it? What happened last night? Dance Club, drinks, letting go, Alejandro. Alejandro! Oh no, I didn't.

Her body jerked up. Her eyes stared at the form next to her. She couldn't see the face, the covers were lying over the head.

The hair.

The hair—it was long, a rich brownish amber. Her hand went swiftly to the sheet, grabbed the edge and yanked back.

Carly rolled over, frowned, yanked on the covers bringing them back over her head.

"Carly!" Jessica's voice was full of surprise and relief.

"What? Who were you expecting?" Bolting upright, Carly turned, faced Jessica. "Alejandro?" Her accent on his name was obvious.

Jessica noticed the way Carly's eyes lit up at the prospect of him in Jessica's bed.

Annoyed, Jessica shoved the blankets aside, swung her legs over the side of the bed. "Don't be silly, of course not." She padded toward the bathroom.

Carly sat up, her arms on her bent knees. "Well I wouldn't mind waking up to him in my bed."

As Jessica entered the bathroom, she stopped first at the sink. Looking at her reflection in the mirror, she remembered how she felt when she thought it was him.

Stop it! You're a business woman, and he's your employee.

Memories of the night before drifted into her mind. Dancing with him, laughing, drinking... coming home? Sticking her head out the door, she addressed Carly, who had laid back down and covered up her head.

"How did we get home?"

The muffled voice spoke. "Taxi."

"Really? And up the stairs?"

"We did that on our own I guess. We're here."

Jessica leaned against the door frame.

Nope don't remember.

"I'm going to take a shower."

Again the low muffled voice. "Knock yourself out."

As the warm water cascaded over her body, visions of bright flashing lights, a pulsating body and smooth cold drinks, many cold drinks, capered through her mind.

Oh, I hope I didn't make a fool of myself. Did I?

Her back hit the shower's tile wall with a thud.

This is not good.

She had to face Alejandro today.

Will it be awkward?

She would be able to tell by his reaction.

Oh well, face your demons.

As she dried off, she tried not to obsess on the events of the night before.

What happened, happened. Deal with it.

Dressed and ready to tackle her day plus whatever else was waiting, she walked back out into the living area. Carly was sleeping, in a peaceful kind of way.

I'll get coffee.

The trip down the stairs was quiet and undisturbed. She hoped not to run into anyone. The familiar sounds of Italian music floated out to greet her. As she rounded the door, she saw the comforting form of Uncle Sal. Her footsteps must have alerted him, as he turned slowly, looking her up and down as a stiff smile played across his face.

"Uncle Sal." She nodded as usual, making a bee line for the coffee.

Her cup was waiting for her as always. Pouring slowly, she kept her back to Sal. He had not replied to her greeting. The silence was like a wall. Taking another cup off the hook, she poured Carly's coffee. Still no sound from Sal. Gathering her courage, she put down the cup, turning to face him. He was standing in the middle of the kitchen, his arms folded across his massive chest.

"Uncle Sal? Am I in trouble?" She felt like a naughty little girl.

"Are you?" His tone was like that of a parent who had just caught his child sneaking in past curfew.

Plopping back against the counter she looked at him with pleading eyes. "I don't know. I can't remember."

His laughter caught her off guard. "Then you probably aren't." He turned back to his pot, chuckling to himself.

Her stance became ridged.

He's messing with me.

"Uncle Sal, have you spoken to Alejandro yet this morning?"

"No, is my nephew in as bad of shape as you?"

"I'm not in bad shape, just bruised a little."

More confused. I can't tell the difference between what happened and what I dreamed.

Uncle Sal's deep baritone joined the song on the radio, but his words were his own. "The lovely lady is confused about what she feels and what she wants."

Coffee sloshed onto the counter as she grabbed up the two cups. Stomping loudly she made her way up the stairs.

Carly bolted upright when Jessica entered the apartment. "What the hell?" Her angry eyes glared at Jessica.

Jessica sat the cups of coffee on the nightstand next to Carly. She could feel the fury inside of her moving up to her face. Even so, as quickly as it came, she lost it.

What am I so mad about? As far as I know, I didn't do anything wrong last night except maybe have some... okay several lustful thoughts.

Her legs gave out and she sat hard on the bed and on Carly's legs.

"Ouch."

"Move over." Jessica shoved at her friend.

When the bed stopped moving, she handed Carly her cup of coffee.

"What happened last night?" She looked at her friend searching for the right answers.

Looking over the rim of the coffee cup, Carly narrowed her eyes.

"Nothing, other than you had a good time, which you needed. What do you think happened?"

Relief washed over Jessica.

Nothing. I did nothing wrong.

"It doesn't matter. Tell me your plan for the café?"

"After my shower." Carly climbed out of the bed on the other side.

* * *

The two women bent over the large paper layout of the café Carly had drawn. Jessica studied her friend's design. She liked the look of it, but then she always was impressed by Carly's visions. The mock-up of the new and improved café was an illustration of black lacquered tables covered in white tablecloths, a single white rose in a cut crystal vase in the middle. Matching black chairs sat on black and white tile laid in an abstract pattern. The bar was the room's center attraction. Floor-to-ceiling mirrors reflected a black lacquered bar shining with crystal glassware and bottles of liquors. The people Carly had drawn were only men, in tight black pants, tuxedo shirts opened to reveal sexy chests.

"Doesn't anyone else work here besides hunky men?" Jessica was a little startled by the complete contrast from her nice authentic Italian eatery.

Carly leaned on the bar and gave Jessica a quizzical look. "Do you want to make money?"

Jessica rose up. "Well... yes."

"Then there needs to be some changes. Upscale and hip will bring in new business, new recognition." Carly was never more vibrant as she was when she was selling an idea.

"All this is well and good Carly, but where will I get the money?" Jessica poked her finger on the pile of bills lying next to the drawing. "The café is doing good, but I still have start-up cost to pay."

Carly leaned on the bar, looking into the large mirror behind it. "We need a hook, something to bring people here." Turning her body around, she again leaned her elbows and back against the bar.

Jessica watched her eyes dart around the room. Knowing Carly's way with ideas, Jessica could almost hear the wheels running in her head. All of a sudden, Carly's head stopped moving. Jessica followed Carly's gaze as it settled on the three men in the corner, working and laughing. Waiting until the silence was unbearable, Jessica finally exploded.

"What?"

Carly cocked her head. "The young studs, what do they do besides work here?"

"They go to college. Roberto is pre-law, Fernando is education and Alejandro's pre-med." Jessica smacked Carly on the arm. "Don't call them 'the studs'. They're more than that."

Carly didn't even flinch. "Have they ever considered modeling? College has got to cost a lot. Modeling pays well."

Jessica's mind wasn't getting a handle on Carly's train of thought. "What does that have to do with me making money here?"

Slowly and easily Carly explained. "I'm working in Milan with the fashion industry."

"Yeah. And?"

What does this have to do with anything?

Jessica stood still as Carly pushed off from the bar, sauntered over to the boys. Her arms on their shoulders, she held their attention with whatever she was telling them.

With her arms folded, Jessica waited for Carly's return. Her curiosity was getting the best of her. In a way, she felt protective of the guys who had come to her aid when she thought it was never going to work out.

Their reactions to what Carly said to them were each different, but mirrored their personalities. Roberto was all excited. Talking a mile a minute, he was ready for whatever challenge came next. Fernando the level headed one, looked skeptical. Alejandro, leaning against the wall, took it all in his easy way. Jessica wondered what the plan was, but she waited. Not patiently, but she waited, nevertheless...

Alejandro looked over at Jessica, he gave her a wink. Biting her lower lip, she smiled back. She still needed to know what went on last night, she just hadn't cornered him by himself. He didn't seem to be acting any differently. With him you couldn't tell. His movements and attitude were always so even. He would make a good doctor. Patients looking into those dark brown eyes would trust him with their life.

Lost in her thoughts, Jessica was startled to find Carly standing in front of her.

"Done deal." The satisfaction on her friend's face was unnerving.

"What's done?"

Carly swung up on a stool, crossed her legs and leaned back on the bar. "Stage one of your road to riches. The boys have agreed to be models."

"And that helps me, how?" Jessica still did not understand the connection.

Carly swung slightly towards her. "Your boys model, they mention working in your café. If you want to see them in action come to *Di Me Sogni*. Wa-lah. Business. Who wouldn't travel to see such fine specimens up close and personal?" She turned back around to admire her new project. "Gawd, I amaze myself."

Jessica's eyes widened. "That's the plan? To use Roberto, Fernando and Alejandro as bait to bring in customers? And they are okay with this?"

Carly laughed softly. "They love it."

The boys were talking, working and looking completely all right with the plan.

Well, okay. Stage one, plan B.

* * *

Jessica approached Alejandro slowly while he was hanging glasses on the rack. The dining room was empty, and she needed to know what had happened the night before.

"Alejandro?" Standing close to him, the smell of his cologne reminded her of last night.

His body turned towards her, his eyes soft and kind. "Si?"

Squirming under his gaze, she searched his face. His expression did not give her a clue as to what his answer was going to be to her question.

Gathering up her courage, she began. "Last night..." She wanted to look away, but she held her head high and straight. "...was I? ...?"

"Enchanting, beautiful... extremely hot." A wicked smile broke across his face, lighting up his mocha eyes.

His words excited her. "Okay about the hot? Just how hot?" Trying to keep her voice calm.

He leaned in whispering close to her hair. "Hot enough to mesmerize every man in the place."

"And us?"

"Us?" Alejandro pulled back looked at her with wicked eyes.

Jessica fumbled for the right words. "Did we... do anything?"

He chuckled. "We danced. We Drank. What more did you want?" His tone tantalized her.

"No, I didn't want any more. I was just afraid I had acted... badly."

"Badly? Explain badly."

"Well..." She narrowed her eyes. "If you don't know what badly is, then I must not have done it."

She just wanted to get away from him. She had made a fool of herself, and he could laugh all he wanted after she was gone. However, one burning question remained. His presence always seemed as if he was looking out for her.

"One more question. Why did you send me home in a cab and not bring me home on your motorcycle?"

His whole face lit up with laughter. "You kept falling off. So I called my cousin, and he took you and Signorina Carly home. I followed on my bike, made sure you got up the stairs."

She couldn't help but laugh. "Fair enough." She had her answers. She turned to leave.

A hand on her arm stopped her. He pulled her to him, his lips almost against her cheek.

"If anything had happened between us, you would have remembered."

The words sent a hot flame down her thighs to her sweet place between her legs. Relaxing against him for a minute, she ran her hand over his strapping chest, lifting one eyebrow.

"So would you."

CHAPTER EIGHT

"Damn."

The loud clap of thunder made Jessica jump. The storm descending on them from the sea was attacking with a powerful anger. As she looked out of the glass in the café's door, she touched the dampness on the window with her fingers. She was glad Carly had left hours ago to return to the city.

Alejandro was just finishing up his shift, everyone else had left. One o'clock in the morning was arriving with a lot of noise and bright flashes of lightening. The wind shook the building so hard it threatened to tear off the café's awnings.

With his jacket on, Alejandro walked over to the front window. Looking out, left and right, he shook his head as he turned to Jessica. "It's going to be a wet ride home tonight."

Jessica had never thought about where Alejandro lived. "How far do you have to go?"

Passing her, he smiled. "Ten, twelve miles. Not far."

Jessica grabbed his arm. "No way. You can't ride in this storm. You're staying here, at least until it blows over."

Looking around, he quipped. "Where will I sleep? On the tables, the floor?" A frown creased his brow. "I think I would fall off the bar."

"Funny boy. Upstairs." Taking hold of his always hot hand, she gave the café one last look around, then led him to the stairway. The steps creaked as she grabbed the rail to go up.

Alejandro jerked her to a stop. "Excuse me. Are you inviting me to your bed?"

As she looked in the dark mink-colored eyes, she had to smile. "As intriguing as that sounds, um, no. I have two apartments upstairs. You can use one."

Slipping her hand from under his, she lifted her skirt and finished the climb. His footsteps followed her. She had to smile.

The idea is... well enticing, but... she looked back at him *...Nice to be considered worthy to share your bed.*

At the landing, she pushed opened the door.

Alejandro's voice came from behind her as she entered her part of the apartment. "Where's my door? I only see the one and..." he looked around the apartment. "...this is yours? Yes?"

"Yes, the other one is over here through the bathroom."

She led him to the bathroom, passed the shower, to the door on the other side. Opening the adjoining door, she stepped into the second apartment. He walked passed her, looked over the living space.

"Quite nice. Thank you. This will be better than riding in the rain."

"We share the bathroom, so knock before entering. The bed linens are fresh, towels are in the cabinet. I can't have my best bartender drowning, now can I?"

His eyes sparkled with a small boy's mischief. "Is that the only reason you asked me to stay?"

She raised her chin. "What would be another reason?"

"Are you afraid of storms?" He moved closer to her.

His breath was sweet on her cheek. "No, not especially."

"If you get frightened..." the dare reflected in his eyes. "...please feel free to come into my bed for comfort."

"Honey, if I ever come to your bed it will not be for comfort." She winked, moved away. Back on her side of the apartment, she shut the door. Leaning against it, she sighed then her mouth eased into a grin she couldn't control.

* * *

The powerful storm slammed against the side of the building. Jessica covered her head. She had tossed and turned most of the night. Only once did the rain fall in a sleep inducing patter against her windows. Her clock said six o'clock in the morning. She really wanted to sleep a couple more hours, but seeing the rain cascade down the windows made her thirsty.

Jessica tossed her covers off, swung her feet over the side of the bed. She sat for a while to get her bearings. Standing, she stretched her arms over her head, then lifted her hair out of her eyes. Then she shuffled to the bathroom to get a drink, not thinking as she turned the handle, pushed opened the door. Startled, she was greeted by a very naked Alejandro stepping out of her shower.

Frozen in her tracks, she let her eyes travel down his body. His shoulders were broad and straight, his chest rippled with muscles. On the side of his six pack stomach was a large colorful tattoo. Her sweep of him stalled for just a second, then continued on to the narrow hips, finally tracing the dark hair leading his pleasure trail to his manhood. If she thought of him as a boy she now knew she was wrong on all counts.

She tried to bring her eyes back up to his face, but they stayed on the fine looking manhood hard and at attention between the two powerfully built thighs. Luckily, she was holding on to the doorway or her knees would have buckled. His voice brought her eyes back up to his face.

Slowly wrapping a towel around his waist, he spoke to her low and sensual. "What happened to knock first?"

"I forgot." The best answer she could get out.

His smile was wicked. "To knock or that I was here?"

"Both." Her words were not flowing well.

He walked over to stand in front of her. "Didn't you hear the shower?"

"With all the pounding rain? No." Her voice barely above a whisper.

His fresh, clean scent, the droplets of water falling from his hair, were all making their way into her senses.

"I'm sorry. Excuse me. I'm really sorry." She stammered as she backed out of the door, a thought came to her. "Why are you up at six anyway?"

"Mass. I go to Mass with my mother."

Her heart stirred at such a noble thought.

Of course you do.

"Sorry. Going." She softly closed the door as if she was trying to leave a sleeping child without disturbing it. Crawling back into bed she dug down into the covers. Her thirst was gone. Her watering mouth had taken care of that.

* * *

The storm made the streets sparkle like a reflection pool. Jessica leaned on her balcony railing, in awe of the full arch rainbow that appeared and disappeared into the sea.

Alejandro had left the apartment soon after she had interrupted him. The vision of him stepping out of the shower was burned in her mind. It was not an unpleasant memory, just disturbing in a desirable sort of way.

Jessica watched the people move about their daily business. She so liked this village by the sea. The new plans were not exactly what she wanted the café to be, but she needed to make money.

Sometimes in life you need to do what you need to do to get from point A to point B.

Knowing Carly as she did, the plan was the best.

I want to stay here. Even if it's alone. I want to stay here on the shores of this sea, in this village, running my café.

"Deep in thought?" Carly's voice cut through her inner voice.

She sighed and turned around. "So, what are you doing back so soon?"

A soft, cool breeze blew Carly's hair, which only made it look better.

"I'm meeting some buyers, hoping your three amigos will make an impression. The word will get around there are men who look like models working at *Di Me Sogni*."

"Good, the boys will impress them." Jessica turned back to the sea view.

Carly's voice sounded closer. "Are you okay with this?"

"Sure. It's a good thing. It's all good." Her heart was not so sure, but her head was.

"If you have qualms..."

Jessica turned around, patted Carly on the arms. "No, no qualms, no problem, just..." She didn't know how to say it. "Make sure they are treated right, okay? They are important to me."

Carly's sincerity was present in her voice. "They'll be helping you. You'll benefit."

"Fine, but not at their expense, okay?"

Carly took Jessica's arm as they walked back into the apartment. "Okay."

* * *

Jessica's desk was piled high, so she took the afternoon to catch up on the bookkeeping. The rat-a-tat of the calculator kept a steady beat for a least an hour. Deep in her thoughts and numbers she was surprised when Sal's hand stopped her fingers.

"Time to eat." Spoken as a command.

Sal didn't remove his hand. Looking up at the big man, they locked eyes, she knew it was eat or he would not leave her alone.

He was right. She had been at it for hours, and anyway the work was done. The figures would not change the facts, only justify them. The café was holding its own but barely. About half as many more customers would get her above water; twice as many would give her an advantage and some breathing room. The locals supported her, but pulling in business from the bigger cities and the tourists, would work wonders.

She stretched, her hands on the back of her hips, as she walked over to the meal Sal had prepared for her.

"Do you think we could handle twice as much business?"

"Of course." No thought or hesitation. As a treat, Sal was joining her. Balancing his large frame on the stool, he speared his salad

The other stool was for her. A lunch of salad, pasta and of course red wine was set.

Pick his brain. He knows the restaurant business.

After sitting down, she leaned forward on the table.

"So Sal, if I can bring in double the business and keep it up for say six months, I could see a real financial future here."

Sal looked at her the way she looked at him when he spoke Italian. "Financial future? What is this financial future?"

With her fork half way to her mouth, she stopped. "Money, successful business..." she waved her hand towards the desk. "...pay the bills, have some left over."

His head followed her waving hands. A frown creased his forehead. "You need money? I give you money. I have lots of money."

Jessica laid her fork down on the edge of the plate.

This dear sweet man.

"No, I don't need money, I want to make money. With the café. Like we are doing, only more."

"Why?" His question was honest. He really didn't understand.

How do I explain?

"Because I need to make money to keep the café. I love the café. I want to stay here and..." Her mind stopped.

Do what? Get married and have kids? Is that still part of the dream?

Tears hit her cheek before she realized she was crying.

The scraping of a stool and the comforting arms of the gentle giant made her tears flow even harder.

"There, there Signora Jessica. It will be all right. Uncle Sal will pay all the bills and give you money and everyone will be happy. Si?"

Unable to speak, she didn't know how to tell this lovely man making money was not what it was about. She thought it was, but it was about having her place in the world. She had made money, knew how to make money. What she wanted was to make a home, a life. Standing up she went into his embrace, letting her emotions flow freely with her tears. The smell of garlic and tomatoes was probably the best smell in the world. Her face buried in Sal's chest gave her a good feeling.

The backdoor slammed, followed by the voice of Alejandro. "What is wrong?"

Freeing herself from Sal's grip, she ran to the dining room. She could not face him right now. Not after seeing him naked now her tears , it was too much for her fragile emotions...

Oh shit.

Making her escape through the kitchen's swinging door, Alejandro's voice followed her as did Sal's.

"What is going on here, Uncle Sal?"

Sal's voice, full of frustration. "I don't know. Money for the future, café, business, then tears, many tears."

Their voices faded as Jessica rushed through the front door. Seeing the sea in front of her, she ran to the rock wall. Reaching it, she grabbed the ledge, bowed her head and just cried. Her shoulders shook. She knew her face was streaked with tears, and she was gasping for breath as the crying took over her body.

What the hell?

Something had triggered this chaotic change in her emotions.

What changed?

Normally she had a handle on things, but this...

This overemotional blubbing fool is out of character. What is your problem girl?

The hands on her shoulders answered her question. The scent of Alejandro and the feel of his body behind her told her what had changed. She wanted to be in his world. She loved the energy, the love his family had for each other, for their lives.

He drew her into him. "Signorina Jessica, what is wrong?"

Laughter swelled up in her, she leaned her head back against his chest.

"Oh, Alejandro."

His breath on her neck sent chills down her back. She had avoided thinking of him as anything other than her bartender, helper, and friend.

Nevertheless, relaxing against him as the sea sent a warm breeze across her face, she let some of her hidden feelings mingle with her suppressed desires. Only she was still his boss, still married.

Now is not the time to let it all out. Maybe someday soon, I can tell him.

His deeply male voice, with exasperation and concern. "What can I do for you? What do you need? Anything, Signorina, anything."

She turned in his arms, to look up into the kindest and most beautiful eyes she had ever seen. "Look, I'm sorry about this morning."

His frown and a look of confusion crossed his face.

"The shower, you. . ." Jessica could not keep her eyes from looking downward. "...naked." She raised her face back up.

The smile wrinkling his face was the sexiest she had ever seen. "Is that why you cry?"

Her shyness seemed to amuse him.

"No, I cry because..." Wiping her eyes with her hand. "...I'm overwhelmed with the kindness of you people. And..." Words failed her.

Alejandro took her face gently in both of his hands. Bringing his lips down to hers, the softness of his lips and the heat of his tongue made her rise up on her tiptoes to meet his kiss. Wrapping her arms around his neck, she gave him all the pent-up desire she had pushed away. As their kiss intensified, she melted into his hard, feel-so-good body. Her thighs were burning. As tender as the kiss was, the underlying heat was unmistakable. When, not if, he made love to her, she would finally know what it was to be pleasured by a passionate lover.

Her body felt him pull back, she reluctantly let go of him along with the images in her mind. The sweetness of the moment brought more tears.

His hands cupped her face again. "Why do you cry?"

Shaking her head, she didn't know how to answer him as she wasn't quite sure of the question.

"I don't know. It's a woman thing." She watched as his eyes clouded over.

His tone was compassionate, indicating a wiliness to listen. "Men would not understand?"

"Honey, women don't always understand." She let the joy of not having to explain level her mood.

He gathered her back in his arms. His deep laughter flowed over her as he swung her back and forth.

"We must get to work." She just wanted to be with him for a few hours, even if it was watching him work.

They wrapped their arms around each other's waist as they crossed the street.

"Are you sure you don't want money? Uncle Sal thinks this is all about money."

She squeezed his ribs.

"Not right now. But tell him to keep the offer open."

* * *

The staff was sitting in the dining room, listening to Carly lay out her plan. "We'll take it in steps and levels." The ever-poised Carly was not winning this crowd over. They sat stoned-faced with their arms crossed looking at her. "Jessica?"

Standing next to Carly, Jessica stepped forward. "Small changes." She put up her index finger and thumb to indicate small.

Everyone nodded and muttered "Si."

Carly's sideways glance to Jessica spoke volumes of frustration, but she continued. "First we will dress the part."

Jessica looked over at the kitchen doors, locked eyes with Alejandro, motioned for him to enter.

Gasps of "ah" filled the air as he strolled out in a white tuxedo shirt, unbuttoned to reveal the beginning of his chest hair, tight black chinos, Italian made loafers. Even Jessica had to draw in a breath at his charm. As he turned around, he winked at her. Spreading his arms, exaggerating his strut. The crowd clapped and hollered.

Carly, striving to regain her composure, got up to speed with her presentation. "For the women, er woman..."

Fiorenza blushed.

"...we have a black skirt and white big shirt, accented by a truly exquisite silver belt and comfy shoes by the finest designer." Laying the outfit on the bar, Carly stepped back as Fiorenza rushed up to grab her new uniform. Jessica smiled at her joy. Carly had pulled in some favors to get a major discount for the new look.

Jessica was so wrapped up in everyone's enjoyment, she was shocked by the next words she heard.

"And for the hostess." Carly whipped out a stunningly beautiful black silk halter top dress, outlined in sparkling studs.

Jessica touched the material. It felt light and smooth as she rubbed it between her fingers. Carly held in her other hand a pair of black, sexy, Italian designer open-toed high heels. Jessica gasped. The whole outfit was unbelievably amazing.

Carly dangled the shoes in front of Jessica. "Go try it on."

Jessica shook her head no, but the demand of the crowd forced her to grab the dress and shoes and run up the stairs.

Once in the bathroom, she stripped down to her underwear. Raising the dress up over her head, she let it cascade down over her body. It was like a silken waterfall touching her skin in luscious waves. Looking at herself in the mirror, she was pleased with her reflection, a curvy body that moved with ease. She tousled her hair and laughed out loud.

You go girl.

Carly had paired Trasparenze thigh high stockings with the shoes. She sat down to put on the stockings and shoes, hoping she didn't fall and break her neck. It had been awhile since she had worn shoes other than flat sandals.

Descending the stairs in full ensemble, she entered the dining room to a chorus of cat calls, whistles and the sexy look in Alejandro's eyes. When she reached the bottom, she twirled and was stopped by his strong arms.

His lips brushed her cheeks as he whispered against her skin. "You are a most beautiful woman, Signorina Jessica."

CHAPTER NINE

The silhouette of the man who walked pass the big front window made the hair on the back of Jessica's neck stand up.

Charles, what the hell are you doing here?

Looking quickly over her shoulder, her eyes swept the room. Alejandro, behind the bar with his back to the room, was straightening the bottles. At the server's station Roberto and Fernando worked quietly together setting up their work area. Tristan, as the head waiter, was overseeing them.

Good, I'll meet him at the door.

Her concern was to shield her café and staff. There was no way she was going to give Charles a chance to criticize. He had no place here. He had walked out. There was no way in hell she was letting him walk back in again.

At the door, she cut him off before he saw her. Her word sharp and biting. "What do you want?"

Jessica saw in his hand he carried a large white envelope. "Jessica, you startled me. Can I come in?" He looked around her into the dining room.

Putting her hand on the doorway, she blocked his entrance. "No."

With her hands on his chest she pushed him back outside away from the customers. It was four o'clock and people had already started to line up on the sidewalk. Jessica figured she had a little less than an hour to deal with Charles and send him away.

But he noticed the line and, being Charles, he wanted to know what was going on. "Are these customers?"

Her stance shifted from one foot to another. "Yes."

Charles looked at his watch. "Are you opening earlier?"

"No." Her eyes bore into his.

A woman in her thirties' interrupted them. "Excuse me is this where the models work?"

Jessica side glanced at Charles. All his attention focused on her as he waited on her answer. "Yes, they work here."

"The models?" It was a predictable question from him. "What's going on here?"

Charles stepped back taking a good look at Jessica. Sporting her new outfit, she saw he was taken aback.

His eyes traveled over her. "You look great."

Ignoring him, she turned her interest to the white envelope. "You have something for me?"

Shrugging he held it up. "I have some papers you need to sign."

She kept her voice flat.

He is not going to get a rise out of me.

"Fine." Jerking them out of his grasp. "Anything else?"

Charles just stood there with his empty hands, but his head moved around to look at the crowd gathering. "The restaurant seems to have taken off. What did you do?"

Her anger was rising.

If he thinks for one moment...

"I stayed and took care of business. Why?"

His head jerked around at her snarky remark. "Fair enough. Look if you can just sign the papers."

"Do you mind if I read them first? Just to protect myself since you seem to like to blindside me."

His shame showed in his face.

As it damn well should.

"Okay, you made your point. I'll come back to-morrow."

Her suspicions surfaced. "What's the rush, Charles?"

Embarrassed, he looked down at the ground.

"Bambi wants to get married."

Jessica would have laughed, if it hadn't been so pathetic. "Is she pregnant?"

Charles let her see the annoyance in his eyes for just a moment, then changed his tone. "No. Her mother doesn't approve of us..."

"...sleeping together?" Jessica spit out at him.

Charles jerked back. "So to speak."

"Well, I wouldn't want to hold up the blushing bride. Come back tomorrow around noon. Get your papers then." Dismissing him, she shooed him away with her hand. "Now go. I have work to do."

Without speaking, he turned to walk down the cobblestone walkway. As he passed the line, Jessica noticed he was summing up the number of people.

Business had increased since the boys had started modeling. The word had spread far and wide, just as Carly had predicted, and the boys enjoyed the work along with the extra money it brought them.

Jessica slapped the papers against her hand. Soon this part of her life would be all over. Italy wasn't big on divorce, so she needed to look the papers over thoroughly.

* * *

As soon as she got a break in the crowd, Jessica slipped back to her desk and opened the white envelope. Educated enough to understand most legal documents, she had an uneasy feeling about just signing them. Looking them over, she was glad Charles had filed in the States. It should make it easier, but she wasn't sure.

Who can I go to for help?

She didn't know any lawyers in Italy.

But...

She turned in her chair as she heard Roberto tell Sal he was taking a break. Watching him stroll through the kitchen and out the back door, she gathered up her papers, and followed him. He was leaning against the building, one leg up behind him, his head back on the stucco wall. As she approached, he turned his head and smiled at her.

"Ahh, the lovely Signorina Jessica. Did you come to run off with me?" His laugh was contagious.

She couldn't help smiling back.

He is a charmer.

"Not this time. I need your help." She pulled the legal papers out, handed them to him.

He took them, looked down at the top page. "Anything for you, my lady." After a few minutes, he looked up at her. "These are American divorce papers?"

Jessica nodded.

Roberto's puzzled look made Jessica nervous. "You don't want the divorce?"

"Oh yeah. I want the divorce."

"You don't like the terms?"

Jessica struggled with how to explain it to him. "I like them. I'm afraid he will change them if I just sign and give it back to him."

"He sees you are doing good business. Maybe rethink his letting you have it all?"

Overjoyed that he understood. "Yes. What should I do to protect myself?"

Roberto slipped the papers back into the envelope. "Let me protect you. When is he coming back?"

"Tomorrow. Noon."

"Stall him. I have an uncle who is a lawyer. Let me have him look at these."

Of course you do.

Before she could stop herself, she threw her arms around Roberto's neck, kissing his cheek. "Thank you, thank you."

His arms went around her waist steadying her. "Anything for you, Signorina Jessica. You have been very good to me. I owe you much."

His kind words made her heart feel good. "You owe me nothing. You saved my ass, all of you boys."

He patted her backside. "And such a nice ass it is."

Pulling back she looked at him with an amused look. Her mind went back to when Alejandro first said the same thing to her.

Are all Italians ready to save a fair maiden's ass? Seems so.

* * *

The night's closing was bittersweet for Jessica. It had been a strange day with Charles showing up. She had felt safe in her little world until the reality of her life hit her in the face. Flipping the switch to turn off the window lights, she leaned against the door frame to watched Alejandro close down the bar. He was quite a guy. She had to smile. At first he was her savior, then her friend and protector. Now, feelings for him as a lover were overtaking her heart.

Is it because of the passionate kiss we shared? Because Charles showed up? Or knowing very soon I'll be free?

Jessica now looked at Alejandro as a man. Not only was he drop dead gorgeous, his spirit was soft-hearted and his manner old-fashioned and chivalrous.

What kind of a future would I have with a pre-med, eventually a doctor? Where does he want to practice? Some big city that would take him away from here?

She frowned.

It may be a pipe dream.

She didn't heard Fernando come up next to her. "Why do you frown?"

Gathering her wits about her, she shook her head. "Nothing." Her attention went from Alejandro and her day dream, to Fernando and the here and now. "What's up?"

Fernando gestured toward the workstation. "We're done, anything else?"

Every night he came to ask the same question. He would not leave until she assured him the work was done. Some nights she needed him to move things, he was always willing. Fernando was the thoughtful one, he would make a fine teacher.

"We're good. Go enjoy what little there is of the night." Bowing he started to turn when she grabbed his arm. "Do you like modeling?"

His smile was crooked, quick. "It's alright. It is helping to pay the bills. Gives me a little to put back for the last year of college. But I like working here better."

"Really? Why, thank you." Before she let go of his arm she had one more question. "Where do you want to teach?"

His brows came together. "Why here in the village, where else?"

"Not a big city or a different country?"

He chuckled. "No, that would be Roberto. He wants to be a big shot lawyer, travel the world."

Hoping she wasn't too obvious. "Alejandro?"

The dimple in his cheek widened. "He wants to stay in the village. Be the best doctor here."

She nodded, releasing him. As he walked away, she scooted over to the bar. Leaning on the counter, she waited until Alejandro noticed her.

His first words took her back. "I saw your husband Charles was here."

Straightening up, she frowned. "How did you know? You've never seen him."

"I saw you talking to a man outside before we opened. Your body language told me you were not pleased to see him. Si?"

"Si." She relaxed. "He was here to give me divorce papers."

He leaned down to her, his breath tickling her nose. "And this is good?"

Her lips could almost brush his. "Yes, this is good."

As he spoke his lips came close. "So why the sad face?"

Oh, god I want to kiss him so badly.

"I'm afraid he'll try to take the café away from me."

This time when he spoke, it was against her lips. "He won't. Roberto will not let him." His mouth yielding, sensual she really wanted to crawl over the bar to be in his arms.

Her lips curled in a smile.

No secrets, oh what the hell.

She put her lips on his, and he teased hers with his tongue. The kiss came slow, bringing a promise of delightful passion. Luckily, she was being held up by the bar, or she would have slithered down to the floor.

For several minutes, they let their kissing tease and tantalize each other. Alejandro was so tender and adorable. But she wanted to inject some desire, so she brought her kiss to a level that showed her hunger. He responded, a smoldering spark sending a heat down her body. When he pulled back, she wanted to collapse. His eyes sparkled with mischief.

His voice rolled over her like a soft rain, "You will someday know my desire for you. It will be a bringing together of two souls."

Even his words could make her loins ache. In a whisper, she had to ask. "When?"

His finger traced her jaw line. "When you feel free of the past." Then he stepped back.

Her eyes searched his face. He was serious. He knew she had unfinished business. He would wait until the time was right to make love to her.

"Fair enough." Standing up straight, she moved to the stairs to go up to her apartment. As she climbed, she felt his eyes on her. When she reached the top she turned. He was gone, only darkness greeted her. The click of the back door told her when he left the building.

* * *

Ready for bed, she remembered he would wait until her light went off. Leaning her back on the wall, she flipped the switch. The soft roar of a motorcycle faded as it left.

She smiled to herself. One day soon, he would not leave. He would stay in her bed for the night.

CHAPTER TEN

Jessica was aware of the peaceful world that had become her existence, the quiet sounds of Sal cooking, the normalcy of finishing her second cup of coffee. Then thoughts of Charles intruded giving her cause to shutter.

A sharp ring from the phone penetrated the stillness. Thinking it was only a call for reservations, Jessica moved the pad to the front of the counter as she picked up the pen. She used her sweetest voice as she answered.

"*Di Me Sogni*. How can I help you?"

Roberto's voice startled her. "Signorina Jessica, you need to come to my uncle's law office. He can get this settled for you."

Excitement welled up in her chest. "Where, when. . .?" She turned to look at Sal. "How?"

"Is Uncle Sal there?"

Sal and Jessica's eyes locked. "Yes."

"Put him on the phone." Roberto instructed her.

She held out the phone to Sal, who was already wiping his hands.

Her voice betrayed her nervousness. "Roberto."

Taking the phone from her, Sal spoke Italian fast and in a constant flow, ending the conversation with "Si." Without speaking to her, he dialed another number and again in the rapid, sharp language, he spoke with authority to the person. Holding her breath, her hands together in front of her face, she waited anxiously. When he finished, he turned and gave her his instructions.

"A cab will take you to Roberto. You will sign... papers and get divorce. This is what you want?"

The glee of knowing this matter was being taken care of by two people she trusted, allowed her to let her whole face smile.

Hugging Sal, she jumped up and down. "Si, yes, oh yes. Thank you. Thank you so much."

A horn told her a cab was had arrived. She grabbed her purse and rushed out the back door.

Sal's deep laugh echoed behind her. "Godspeed, Signorina Jessica. Godspeed."

The trip was speedy and nerve-racking. A couple of times Jessica closed her eyes and prayed she'd live to sign the papers. The cab screeched to the curb, she saw Roberto waiting. He opened the door, took her arm to help her out. His smile lifted her spirits, but did not calm down her rapidly beating heart. He led her into a quaint store front office. A bell on the door signaled their arrival.

A handsome gentleman stood up to greet her. "Signora Jessica." His accent smooth and light. "I am Lucca Giordano. Roberto is my nephew. Salvador my brother."

Jessica liked him. His eyes showed warmth like the rest of his family. "Thank you, Mr. Giordano, for taking the time to help me."

His smile was bewitching. "Call me Lucca. It's a pleasure to be able to serve you. You are part of our family. We take care of our own."

He took her hand, guiding her to a table with four chairs the papers lying on top. As he pulled a chair out for her, she sat and looked up as Roberto took a chair across from her, Signore Giordano sat next to her. Wanting this to be over with no pitfalls, she waited for them to tell her what to do

Lucca leaned over the papers in front of him. "Now, as I understand from Roberto, you are agreeable to these terms. Your husband has asked to be released from all duties of the café, leaving you all debts, assets and everything, correct?" He raised his eyes to her.

Jessica nodded. Resting her hands on the table, she held them together to stop the shaking. Her nerves were doing a dance in her body. Never before had she been on the verge of a decision that so badly needed to go her way before.

His kind eyes returned to the papers, folding a page over.

"He does not want to pay you anything, like a buy-out, alimony, nothing. Is this what you want?"

Clearing her throat, her words came out choppy. "Yes... I just want the café...I don't want him to ever be able to take it from me."

"Well then, may I ask why you are concerned?"

"I am afraid he'll change his mind. With the help of Roberto, Fernando, Alejandro and especially Sal, we have made the restaurant quite successful. Charles thought it was a money pit, but I have brought it up beyond that." Her voice rose, she thumped herself in the chest,

Damn it Charles, this is mine.

Roberto chuckled and Lucca took her hand and patted it.

"Then we will do this. Sign here. I will fax the copies to his lawyer immediately. Ask him to expedite them."

He slid the papers in front of her. Without hesitation, she scrawled her signature on the paper.

"Wait a moment. You are to meet him today?" The alarm in his eyes sent a queasy sensation to her stomach.

"Yes...at noon." Jessica shot a look over to Roberto.

Lucca leaned forward. "This will take a couple of days. Can you stall him?

Her eyes darted to Roberto. He nodded.

A couple of days. I'll think of something.

Her tone was firm. "Yes."

Lucca's smile was kind and comforting. He gathered up the papers, stood. "Let me get these faxed."

As he left, Jessica turned her attention to Roberto. "You are amazing. I don't know how to thank you."

Roberto leaned back in his chair. "Live happy, Signora Jessica. Find love and have many children."

Jessica laughed.

It was my plan. Still is. Charles' returning did not change that.

"I will. Thank you."

His wink made her feel the warmth of his friendship.

Lucca returned, sat back down at the table. "It is done. Here are the originals with the fax confirmation. And a thank you from his lawyer. Once they are filed in American courts, if Charles would decide to change anything he would have to fight you in Italian courts. It would cost him much money." He finished by rubbing his fingers together.

Jessica took the papers as if they were precious gold. To her they were. Rising from the chair, she held out her hand to the helpful lawyer, but then decided to hug him. His firm embrace let her know she was in good and honest hands.

Roberto came around the table and slapped Lucca on the back. "Thanks Uncle Lucca. Signora Jessica?" He bowed to allow her to go first.

Linking her arm in his, she nodded to Lucca. Roberto guided her out the door, the soft tinkle of the bell followed them.

Stepping outside, Jessica thought the strong Italian sun seemed so much brighter today, now that she was two days closer to being free. Then, she saw him leaning on his cycle, his arms crossed.

Alejandro.

His dark glasses and his stern face told her something was wrong.

Walking up to him, she placed her hands on his folded arms. "What's wrong?"

He unfolded his arms, placed his hands on her waist.. "Charles is at the café. He has a bag and says he's staying until he figures out how well *Di Me Sogni* is doing." He looked over her head at Roberto. "How long until the divorce is final?"

"A couple of days. We have to keep him from thinking too much about changing the terms."

Alejandro bit his lower lip. Jessica stood looking back and forth between the two men. Her mind was blank.

How can I do this? What should I do?

Roberto spoke in quick Italian. Alejandro answered with the same sharp words.

Jessica held up her arms, stepping back out of his hold. "Stop. Tell me what you are saying?"

Her look settled on Alejandro. He stared into her eyes. "We were thinking of getting you away from the café until Uncle Lucca has the final papers."

She folded her arms. "And just where are you planning on sending me?"

Her eyes flitted between them. Both shrugged their shoulders. "Great. I'm staying put."

Alejandro shook his head. "Not a good idea. He is planning on staying in your apartment."

The idea hit her like a bolt of lightning. "Not if someone else is staying there already."

Alejandro frowned. "Who?"

She heard the puzzlement in his voice. Running her hands around his waist, she smiled in a calculating way. "You."

A smile broke across his face as understanding settled in. "You want to use me to make him think there is something going on?"

"Is that all right?"

Throwing back his head, he laughed boldly. "That is so all right."

His arms gathered her into him as he spoke over her head to Roberto. "See what a smart woman I have picked. Brilliant."

* * *

When Jessica walked through the back door into the kitchen with just Roberto, the staff was working quietly, no chatter, no laughing. They glanced up at her, then went back to their tasks. Sal was not singing.

Alejandro went to get some things for their sleep over. His agreement with her plan was perfect. Charles would have to stay somewhere else.

She walked over to Sal, up on her tiptoes, balancing herself with her hands on his shoulders, she whispered into his ear. "Where is he?"

Sal did not stop stirring the creamy white sauce in the pan. "The dining room. How long is he going to be here? I don't like him."

Jessica patted his back. "I don't like him either. But we have to keep an eye on him for a while. We have a plan."

"We?" Sal looked over at Roberto putting on his apron. "You and Roberto?"

"He's in on it. Trust me, it's a good one. Just follow our lead." Jessica chuckled, moved out to the dining room. Charles stood behind the bar looking over things.

"Charles." Her voice startled him, he almost dropped the bottle he was holding. "What are you doing here?"

Regaining his composure, he straightened his shoulders. "Just checking things out. You don't mind, do you?"

"As a matter of fact I do. You walked away. Why do you care?"

"I still have an interest in the business." Charles' arm swept around the room. "You've taken care of things really well.

Her anger roared up, but she worked hard at keeping it from raising its ugly head. If he suspected anything, he could prolong the divorce. That was the last thing she wanted.

"Fine. Look around." She dismissed him as she turned around. But his next words brought a smug smile to her face.

"I thought I would stay in the other apartment, no need to rent a room."

Slowly, she turned, the smile still there. "Well you see. . ."

The swinging kitchen door burst open.

"Darling." Alejandro's voice echoed in the large empty room. He came swiftly to her, put his arm around her waist and kissed her on the cheek. "Sorry I was delayed. I needed to pick up some more things." His eyes traveled to the man standing behind his bar. "Oh, excuse. You are?"

Jessica patted Alejandro's chest in a flirty, intimate way. "Honey, this is Charles, my deserting husband. Charles, this is Alejandro. And, as I was explaining, there is a problem with you staying in the apartment. That's where Alejandro stays."

Charles' look of shock changing to disgust was worth every bit of joy she felt.

"He's living with you? In our apartment? Really Jessica. That's highly improper."

That did it.

Her body went rigid. She felt her face flush. Alejandro's hands holding her arms were the only thing keeping her from scratching out his eyes.

"Don't go there, Charles. Our apartment? It stopped being 'our' apartment when you left with bimbo Bambi."

Alejandro's hold on her was tight as he brought her back into his body. "Easy."

Keep it cool, girl.

"Charles, you need to make other arrangements." She turned her cheek to Alejandro. "Can you let me go now?" Speaking between clenched teeth.

His low chuckle and yielding hold, let her know he was with her all the way. "Don't kill him. Our plan is much better."

Turning in his arms, she kissed his cheek, pinched his ribs then moved towards the kitchen. Looking back when she reached the door, she saw the two men glaring at each other.

Oh this is going to be an interesting few days.

* * *

When Jessica finally closed the café on this very complicated day, she sighed. Charles had hung around getting in everyone's way.

Alejandro had firmly claimed his bar leaving Charles at loose ends. Charles moved about bugging the wait staff and the kitchen staff. They shuffled him from one spot to another to keep him out of their way. Finally, when the customers cleared out and the cleanup started, he plopped down at the bar. Asking for a glass of wine, he sat eating the garlic bread chips, keeping an eagle eye on Alejandro.

Jessica walked over to the bar, going behind it to stand by Alejandro. She wanted Charles gone, but if she showed her hand, he would get suspicious. "So Charles, what do you think?"

Charles' eyes narrowed. "Business looked good tonight, but it could be a fluke."

A fluke! Worked my ass off and he thinks it's a fluke!

She felt Alejandro's breath on her neck, could almost feel him caution her.

"You're right. It's not always like this."

Sometimes it's better.

The wait-staff came over to the bar.

"All done. Ready to lock up." All eyes turned to Charles.

Charles got the hint. Rising from the stool he hesitantly moved away from the bar. "Well, good night. See you tomorrow."

She bristled. "If you must."

Looping her arm through Alejandro's, she guided him to the stairs. Speaking back over her shoulder. "Boys, will you see Charles out?"

Up the stairs they climbed and went into her apartment. Letting her guard down for the first time today, she plopped back on her bed.

She threw her arms over her eyes. "Gawd, I will be glad when he's gone."

Rising up on her elbows, she scrutinized Alejandro, who was smiling as he observed her. "Thank you for helping me out. You are my life saver."

Lessening the space between them, he bent down to kiss her. "Sweet dreams, my lady. Sleep well."

As he stood up towering over her, she felt her heart leap into her chest.

Fat chance that is going to happen.

CHAPTER ELEVEN

Jessica tossed back and forth in bed, the sleep she willed to engulf her never came. The fact Alejandro was in the bed next door made burning, reckless, wanton desire flood across her body. The room felt sultry, suffocating. She kicked off the covers, feeling the warm sweat rise on her clammy skin. Her dampened hair clung to her face, she pushed it away. Her boxer shorts and tank top were moist with perspiration.

Finally, unable to stop the passion that demanded satisfaction, she left her bed and went out on the balcony into the cool night. Leaning on the rail, she weighed her options.

One: Seeing Charles today made her accept that part of her life was over. He had moved on and so should she. Divorcing him would bring closure. She was good with that.

Two: Her mission was to keep the café and stay in this peaceful village. It was her dream and she would not allow it to fade away. If Charles wanted a fight, he would get it. In the last few months she had learned to make it on her own. He had underestimated her as he always had.

Surprise.

Three: Just the thought of it made her knees weak. Her hands grabbed onto the banister, the flowing flames of desire clawed at her, hot and sharp. A trail of fiery passion crept over her. She wanted Alejandro.

Now. Instant gratification.

The cool sea air whispered across the heated flush in her body.

Recalling the memories of him coming out of the shower caused her to scold herself. Not only was his body amazing, the look in his eyes still remained in her thoughts. His dark eyes had smoldered with an unspoken promise of heated pleasure.

The gentle whoosh of the sea on the rocks took her to a fictitious place. Her body responded as if he was touching her, allowing her to fulfill her fantasy. She arched as the sweet longing for him capsized over her breast. The inferno traveled down her ribs to her stomach and settled in her loins. So on fire she thought of just going in and jumping his bones.

What's stopping you? You're an adult, so is he. No, I must use all my will power and stay on course. Go back to bed. This will pass.

The creak of the floorboards caused her to jerk around, she saw him in the shadows moving towards her. Clad only in his pj bottoms, she glanced down at his bare feet. Her gaze traveled up his legs to his bulging sex, hidden from her eyes by a thin piece of fabric. Conscious she was staring, she dragged her eyes up to his face. A jolt of sexual energy rocked her to the bone as distinctive warmth flooded the area between her legs.

"Jessica? Is something wrong?" His deep accented voice only made her hotter.

Biting on her lower lip, she sucked up her courage. She decided it was time for the truth. "I want you."

His brow wrinkled. "To do what at this hour?"

A half laugh huffed out as awareness filled her every pore, even the air she breathed. Her mind wandered imagining his skin warm to her touch, his muscles solid and hard. This was the moment of reckoning.

"I want to make love to you. Now." The words came out easier than she expected.

His eyes locked with hers in a powerful slam as he eliminated the distance between them. A low moan of surrender slipped passed her lips, a husky, helpless sound of want as his body closed in. Jessica gripped the wrought iron railing for support. Alejandro's arms encircled her waist, bringing her into him. She felt their bodies melt together in perfect form. The smell of night dew entangled with her reasoning and the strong smell of his freshly soaped skin.

"Are you sure, Signorina?" His deep masculine baritone murmured in her ear.

"Oh, yes. I'm sure." Her hands glided up his sexy, sculpted abdomen, stopping at the tattoo. "This is beautiful. Does it mean something?"

His soft laughter was a low rumble. "No, it's just a design. And to get it was a dare."

He lowered his mouth, slowly, lazily, never breaking eye contact. His look was like fire and ice. Tasting his lips, she heard him groan as their tongues touched. Her arms slid around his magnificently muscled back, the sinful movement of his hips made her body practically convulse with sexual sensations.

As he deepened the force of his strong, hard lips, she pressed her over-aroused body against him.

He walked her backwards into the apartment, all the while his hands stroked her. The heat of him flowed through her, lashing her skin and stirring her hunger. His hands caressed the lines of her back down to the first hint of her buttocks. Jessica wanted to be closer to him.

Want him in me.

When her legs struck the bed, she fell back bringing Alejandro with her. His powerful, strong, inflamed body loomed over her. Her back arched. Her thighs opened.

Jessica didn't think of the consequences of what she wanted to do. For months she had felt undesirable. Only Alejandro had made her feel like an attractive woman. His flashing brown eyes and electric smile had slowly layered up her feelings for him.

When Charles first left her, it bewildered her that she felt an attraction for another man. But tonight she needed Alejandro to end her want. If he did not take away her longing for him, she would never be able to concentrate.

"My lovely lady." His adoring voice was mesmerizing, filled with potential.

Her stomach felt tight, tense. His words washed over her like an inviting waterfall. His lips moved down her body. She grabbed his rich thick hair with both hands, her body curved to meet his mouth. His tongue left a trail of hot fire-spiked kisses. His hands slipped under her tank top. As he moved the material from her skin, he cupped her breast. Her nipples hardened. A spike of white heat shot down to her center.

Again his mouth was on her. His hands skillfully moved over her ribs to the top of her boxer shorts. Smooth, talented fingertips tickled under the fabric shifting the pants down. As the cool air hit her warm skin, she felt the start of her climax. Never had she come so quickly. She didn't want it to be over too soon. But...

Oh god.

He aroused her to volcano-sized heat that threatened to explode, sending her to the ceiling. Like hot molten lava, the firestorm came on her, filtering down, compelling her body to twist until she felt his hardness. She opened up for him.

His eyes laughed, as his voice whispered. "Be patient my little one. The spark must be fanned and allowed to consume you. You must feel it in your soul."

Her arms dropped to her side. Grabbing the sheets, she held on. This was going to be the ride of her life.

Viva l'Italiano!

Her body exploded with a rush of ecstasy she had not experienced before. Alejandro was skillfully touching his mouth to all her erogenous zones. Not rushing, he kept her body ablaze. She was torn between wanting the big O to explode, leaving her drained or the build up to last forever. No, truthfully she wanted both. And she had the feeling Alejandro knew how to make that happen. For his age, he knew his way around a woman's body. This was no slam, bang thank you ma'am. This was being pleasured until she was satisfied. And she had no doubt she would be pleasured as never before.

Her orgasm started to peak. She begged him, "Please."

He held above her. Her hands clawed at his chest. He took both her wrists, pinning her arms above her head as he entered her slowly. Her womanhood opened up to him and then gripped his hardness. The wave of ecstasy engulfed her bringing a scream from her lips. Her body had never felt such a release.

She felt his climax and then another one of hers joined his. Her legs clamped around his waist as her hips rose up from the bed to take in more of him. He pushed in and then pulled out. Each thrust gave her a new climax. Finally, it released her, with a fulfillment that felt like it would last her a lifetime.

God it's been a long time since I enjoyed sex this much.

The sweet scent of sweat and sex tangled with the salt air coming in the open door was the best fragrance. The drops from his hair touched her lips, leaving a salty taste. As he pulled himself out, her body's grip on him created a tantalizing friction. Rolling from her, she missed his heat, the weight of his body.

She pushed her hair away from her face. Alejandro was curved beside her. His fingertips traced her skin in sensual circular motions. His face was as handsome as ever. Reaching up, she wiped the moisture from his perfect cheek bones. Her fingers cupped the back of his neck. Pulling his head down, she kissed him, a full, long, slow kiss that clouded her mind.

Where do we go from here?

Alejandro outlined the shape of her mouth with the tip of his tongue before stealing another kiss. Her world was in all the right places in his arms.

"Hey, that was so good..."

He stopped her words with another kiss. "You don't need to explain. I have wanted you since the first time I rounded the corner of the alley. The pretty signora in need of a bartender."

She propped up on her elbow. "You never said anything."

His lovely laughter tickled her nose. "What could I say? You needed my help. I needed to help you." He shrugged and hugged her tighter. "I knew we would be together, in time. Your time. So I waited."

She nestled into his strong, firm body. He felt rich with muscles, his caramel skin still glistened with the moisture clinging from the lovemaking. His embrace was comforting and felt as though she had found a resting place.

He started to get off the bed, but she stopped him with her hand on his arm. "Don't go. Stay the rest of the night in my bed."

He smiled as she stood up and wrapped her arms around his waist. He picked her up and tossed her gently on the bed. She scooted over just enough to let him in. Together, they snuggled down into the covers.

The French doors were still open allowing the cooling sea breeze to fill the room. His naked body was all the warmth she needed.

A thought struck her. Her clock said two o'clock. "Do you have to get up early for Mass?"

His chuckle vibrated her body. No, tomorrow is Wednesday. I don't go to Mass on Wednesday."

"Good, then let's sleep in. I haven't slept in for months."

Plus, I want to stay in your arms as long as I can.

"Jessie, you can sleep as long as you want. I will hold you." His voice was like liquid brandy burning, yet smooth.

It was the first time she had heard him call her a nickname not preceded with Signorina.

Sleep washed over her. Her contentment at its fullest. "Don't leave."

The last words she heard put her soul at peace.

"I won't."

CHAPTER TWELVE

For two days Jessica played the game. Charles would arrive at some point in the day and stay until she shooed him out. He made known he was not happy about her living arrangements, but she didn't care. He hadn't asked for her approval when he went off with Bambi. Between Alejandro and herself, she kept her temper in check. No more flying dishes. Charles' displeasure gave her great satisfaction, causing her to chuckle inside.

Alejandro stayed in the other apartment, but at night he slept in her bed. She explored all the things about Alejandro that made her feel giddy, safe and hot. It was a magnificent journey.

As she rubbed her hands over his tat after fierce love-making, her question was out before she could stop it. "Where are we going with this?"

"Where do you want it to go?" He leaned back to look at her face.

Alejandro traveled his index finger down Jessica's arm, over her stomach, up her breast, creating a sweet tingling she never wanted to stop. Drowning in his delightful touch, she succumbed into the moment, and then grabbed his wandering hand. There were some questions she needed to ask him.

"We need to discuss some things."

"Such as?" A wicked smile played at his lips.

"Us." She had to move away from him, his wonderful body heat made it hard to concentrate.

He rolled to his side, raised his head, propping it in his hand. "What about us?"

Jessica sat cross-legged on the bed, a thin sheet lay across her legs. Looking at who was probably the love of her life, she was leery of stepping out of her safety zone to approach the subject.

"Does it bother you that I'm older than you?"

His lips twitched. "How much older?"

Jessica had to smile at that one. "A few years."

His laugh made his eyes twinkle. "No, it does not bother me."

He let his fingers play with her legs, going under the thin material to touch her skin, again bringing her pleasant sensations.

Clamping her hand down to stop his movement. "The future?"

Even her grip could not keep his hand from massaging her skin. The daring look in his eyes let her know she was more serious than him.

"What do you want for the future, Jessie?"

Nervously, Jessica bit her lower lip, looked straight into his eyes,. "Would it scare you off if I said I wanted marriage, children, to settle here in this village, grow old with someone?"

Throwing his head back, he laughed a full-bodied laugh. "I do not see a problem." Alejandro's intriguing eyes hinted at his love for her. "No. That would not scare me off. That's what I want too."

"With me?" Jessica asked the one important question.

A look came to his eyes making her think maybe she was walking on thin ice.

His dark eyes took her into his gaze. "Yes, I want those things with you."

Jessica almost jumped up and down on the bed. "Really?"

His eyes flashed that Alejandro look. "Really. Now enough talk."

His hands traveled up her side, bringing her into his arms as he folded her into him. "Sleep. Everything will be good."

* * *

As Jessica and Alejandro enjoyed their morning coffee at the table in the kitchen, Sal began singing and chopping. When the back door slammed, all three turned to see who had entered. Carly stood bathed in the morning sun light in all her splendid glory.

The joy at seeing her made Jessica jump off the stool, running to embrace tightly her good friend.

Carly pulled back and noticed the tears forming in Jessica's eyes. "What's wrong?"

Jessica wiped her face on the towel she had in her hand. "I'm just so glad to see you. It's been a strange few days. Your face is a welcome sight."

Carly's sereneness touched Jessica. "Tell me, darling."

Alejandro gave up his stool and slid it back for Carly. As she sat down, he placed a cup of rich, hot coffee down for her.

Jessica leaned back in her seat. "Well, Charles showed up."

"Why?"

"He had divorce papers for me to sign." She explained the trip to the lawyer and the delay of a couple of days. "So we are trying to discourage him from wanting the café. But he just hangs around."

Carly sipped her coffee. "How are you discouraging him?"

Jessica winking over at Alejandro. "Well, we made him stay at his hotel..."

"Wait, where did he want to stay?" Carly frowned.

"Here, up in the apartment. So Alejandro moved in and..."

Carly lifted one of her perfectly shaped eyebrows. "Alejandro moved in? I wish I could have seen the look on Charles' face when you told him."

Jessica had to laugh. "It was kind of priceless."

Carly's face lit up with laughter. "So where are we now?"

"Waiting for a judge in the States to sign the decree before Charles changes his mind and wants to revise the terms."

One of Carly's slender brows arched in amusement. "So, waiting is the order of the day. Okay."

* * *

Catching up with Carly was a good way to pass the time. Carly excused herself once to go outside to talk on the phone. No sooner had she returned the kitchen phone rang.

Jessica brushed Alejandro's arm in a loving touch as she went to answer it.

"Roberto." She turned to look at the group of concerned friends whose eyes were on her. Listening closely she nodded. "I'll be right there."

On cue Alejandro took the phone from her, spoke in Italian, ending with his usual 'Si'. No sooner had he hung up than a horn sounded in the alley.

Jessica grabbed her purse, kissed him on the cheek. "How do you do that?" She whispered as he scooted her out the door.

The ride in the cab was like Déjà Vu, the same driver, the same quick trip to the same quaint office. Roberto waited again on the sidewalk.

Hurrying her inside, she tried to talk. "What happened?"

"Your divorce came through. Uncle Lucca called."

Lucca greeted them, coming from behind his desk.

"You, Signorina Jessica are a free woman. Your papers are filed, sealed and delivered." He handed her the white envelope.

Grasping the envelope to her chest, Jessica felt the weight of the last few days lifted from her as she hugged the lawyer.

"Thank you so much for getting this done so fast." She was gushing, but she didn't care.

Awkwardly Lucca smiled. "I didn't do it. It came across the fax. 'Sorry for the delay. Give Jessica my best. Judge Murray.'" Jessica laughed. Pete Murray had been one of Carly's former suitors.

Outside, Roberto handed Jessica a helmet. She laughed as she put it on, clutching the papers of her newfound freedom. Climbing on the back of the bike, she settled into the comfort of the leather seat. Roberto easily guided the cycle through the traffic, down the cobblestone roads.

With the wind caressing her face, Jessica was ready for anything Charles would throw at her.

Bring it on Charles, baby. I am ready to make my own future. .

* * *

As Roberto and Jessica walked in the back door of the café, they were greeted by Sal, Carly, Fernando and Alejandro. She realized how blessed she was to be among such fine supporters.

Carly grabbed her and gave her a huge hug. Pulling back, she searched Jessica's face. "Is it all done?"

Jessica nodded. "All but dropping the bombshell on Charles."

Carly rubbed her hands together. "Oh, I'm so glad to be here for this."

Looking over Carly's shoulder, she saw Sal with his arms around Roberto and Fernando. Alejandro stood leaning against the counter. His sexy smile reinforced her grand feeling of things to come.

A hush fell over the group as all eyes looked beyond Jessica. Turning slowly, she saw Charles standing in the doorway. Still holding the precious divorce papers, she straightened to face him.

Carly put her hands on Jessica's shoulder, pulled her back slightly so she could whisper. "Need backup?"

Jessica smiled, squared her shoulders. "No, I can handle this."

Charles stood there awkwardly. The look on his face said he realized he had entered hostile company.

As Jessica stepped away from Carly, she motioned Charles to go back out the door. "Charles, let's take a walk and talk."

Once outside, Jessica led the way towards the sea wall with Charles shuffling behind her. The bright and crisp day matched the feeling of her soul.

One of the best days of my life.

Reaching the wall she turned to Charles. "I signed the papers. You're free. No strings, no attachments. It will be like it never happened."

"Well..." Charles started. "I think we need to re-think some things. I shouldn't have been in such a hurry. I didn't think of... some things."

"Like what?" Jessica half sat, half stood against the rock barrier.

Charles paced, stopping to face her. "Well maybe we could remain partners in the café. You were right. It is a great business venture. I'm sure Bambi and I could work with you for the good of all."

Jessica so badly wanted to scream uncontrollably at him. But she had lost control when he first left. No, this time she would remain calm, striking a deadly blow.

"I don't think so, Charles."

His voice took on an angry edge. "Well, we'll see. I'll talk to my lawyer." He flipped open his cell phone. "Just because you signed the papers doesn't mean it's a done deal. They need to be filed in a U.S. court..."

Jessica grinned. "Done."

Charles pushed buttons on his phone. "Well...well a judge needs to sign them."

"Done." She took in a deep breath, released it quietly.

The outraged look on his face gave her immeasurable pleasure. Jessica relished in her moment. "It's done Charles. You have your freedom and Bambi, and I have my café and my future without you. Win-win, don't you think?"

The strained silence between them told her he was at a loss for words. Jessica had never seen him speechless. It was a reward in itself. Pushing herself off the wall, she moved around him. Leaving him standing there with his cell phone in his hand along with his tattered dignity.

She pushed the front door open, finding her café world in full swing, like a fine-tuned clock. Sal was in the kitchen singing opera, Roberto and Fernando were at the tables setting them up. Carly sat at the bar with a wine glass in her hand. Alejandro worked away behind the bar. All activity stopped as the doorbell signaled her entry. Five sets of eyes turned to her.

A big smile broke across her face. "It's done."

Throwing her head back, her laughter mixed with the other shouts and claps. Setting her sights on Alejandro, she ran briskly towards him, around the bar. Reaching him, she drew him to her by the front of his shirt, pulling his head down to hers. Her lips pressed against his with all the passion she had kept below the surface of her heart. His arms went around her, their bodies melting into each other. The force and length of the kiss brought screeches, roars of laughter, clapping.

She had found her spot. In his arms, in her life.

Sometimes when dreams change it's for the good.

When they finally parted lips, she ran her hand down his arm and took his hand. Over his shoulder she looked at Carly.

"Do you think you could handle the café tonight? I need to take the night off."

Alejandro cupped her chin in his hand, laying a soft sweet kiss on her lips. "Yes, you do." His voice was deep and passionate. "Are you okay after all that's happened today?"

"I am more than okay. I am fantastic."

"Then we will celebrate a future of us."

Jessica's heart swelled with the love she had for him. The future looked good.

Really good.

Made in the USA
Coppell, TX
24 August 2022

81973092R00075